THE HOUSE ON HURLEY POND ROAD

Author: Darren Fitzgerald
Editor: Scott Stanton
Designer: Michael Burke
Publisher: Deadbolt Productions LLC

Printed in the United States of America

First Paperback Printing: March 2009

ISBN 978-0-578-01964-2

To my parents,
Patricia and Barry,
and my Goddaughter Kristeen

Contents

FOREWORD

PREFACE

INTRODUCTION

1. The Angel and the Troll   11

2. Dark Waters   29

3. Shadows in the Mist   35

4. A New Beginning   49

5. Ouija Board   65

6. Writing on the Wall   73

7. Home for the Holidays   87

8. Our New House   105

9. The Terror Returns   111

10. The Break-In   119

11. The New Residents   127

12. Death of a Friend   139

13. Down by the River   145

14. Endgame   153

AFTERWORD

FOREWORD

Over the years I have read a great deal of boring 'true' ghost stories who's plots and situations all seem to blend into one long winded oration on cold spots, footsteps and other pranks played by various apparitions. This book however took me by surprise simply by the level that this particular ghost/demon/poltergeist was willing to make itself known.

This is Darren Fitzgerald's first outing as an author and sometimes it shows but it's always refreshing to hear the story directly from the person who experienced the events. Darren does not waste any time overwriting his experiences and is able to get right to the meat of the supernatural occurrences as they happened. Furthermore, this book has a definite beginning, middle and chilling end which most books based on "true" events do not.

I've actually had the pleasure to talk to Darren about his past on several different occasions and some of the events might seem to reach the 'tall tale' level for the average reader. I thought the same until I was able to meet with other members of his family who were able to recall the same events in the same exact way, without prompting.

Darren does a nice job of making you wonder what's going to happen next so you'll probably be able to read through this book in a single sitting, all the way through to its tragic ending.

Whatever the reason was for the Fitzgerald family to be targeted like this is beyond me but my heart goes out to them.

Jacob Mitchell
Paranormal Investigator

PREFACE

Before you dive headlong into this intriguing tale of the supernatural, I owe you a few explanations of what you're about to read, along with some notes of acknowledgement to thank the many individuals who made this project come to life.

First off, a number of the names contained within this novel have been changed to protect the people who we either couldn't find or would rather remain nameless.

The events contained herein are true to the best of my memory, however the first few chapters along with the afterword are fictionalized accounts of actual events. The murders and suicides that these chapters are based on are unfortunately true to the best of my knowledge.

The actual location of the house on Hurley Pond Road will forever remain a secret out of respect to the current and previous owners who may or may not have had any paranormal experience while living there.

As far as acknowledgements go, I'd like to thank first and foremost, my good friend Scott Stanton for his superb work in editing this novel and at times "ghost writing" entire portions of the story itself.

Secondly I'd like to thank my friend of over thirty years, Michael Burke, who's original cover artwork and book design gave this project the initial lift that it needed to get off the ground. Members of his design company Solari Creative were instrumental in building and designing the website (Keith Schoeneick) and directing and filming the trailer (Chris Adornato) which appears on the front page of our website. I'd also like to thank my niece Kristeen for her participation and hard work in the trailer itself.

Lastly I'd like to thank my sister Coreen who experienced the bulk of these supernatural events with me as we were kids. I owe her a world of gratitude.

INTRODUCTION

I decided to write this novel after taking note of the high level of interest that the public was displaying towards anything labeled paranormal these days. Tales of ghosts, poltergeists and hauntings are talked about freely without any consequence of the storyteller being labeled as "crazy".

After viewing the current crop of TV shows such as *Ghost Hunters*, *The Ghost Whisperer*, and *Scariest Places on Earth*, I decided that it was high time to let the public in on what the paranormal meant for my family and I. For us, it was more than just the random turning on of a light fixture or a chair moving across the floor. For our family it was a truly menacing and malevolent force that could cause serious harm and wanton destruction at a moments notice.

Although I could have written this book more than twenty years ago, I don't think that it would have had the same impact as I hope it will today.

I have decided that now is the time to finally tell my family's story.

Enjoy,
Darren Fitzgerald

CHAPTER ONE

THE ANGEL AND THE TROLL

Springtime had arrived early to the small, quaint, coastal villages located near the eastern shore of New Jersey circa 1952. It was a peaceful area, frequently used for retirement purposes, less than a few miles off the Atlantic Ocean. Just far enough away from the beach to avoid the tourist filled crowds that descended on the area like a swarm of locusts each and every summer.

A local businessman named Edgar Strain, was about to take advantage of the unseasonably warm weather by doing some house hunting in this up and coming neck of the woods. After years of congested city living, he felt it was time to move his growing family into larger quarters. His trucking company was thriving and Edgar felt he could afford a larger, more comfortable house with a few acres of land, maybe even a barn where he could build a workshop.

After scouring the real estate ads, he came across a listing that seemed almost perfect – a five bedroom house set on 15 acres of lightly wooded farmland that included a large horse barn and stable. The estate was much larger than Edgar could normally afford, but it was being offered at such a reasonable price that he felt compelled to give it a look. Edgar immediately called a realtor and arranged a walkthrough for that coming weekend.

Saturday morning quickly arrived and found Edgar Strain driving down Hurley Pond Road alongside Frank Sampson, the town's local real estate agent situated behind the steering wheel. They chatted about everything from the weather to the war in Korea, until Frank abruptly turned onto a gray crushed stone driveway and said "Well, what do you think?"

motioning toward the stately manor house.

Edgar was elated – it was just what he had been looking for. "This is fantastic!" he exclaimed as he jumped out of the car and nearly ran to the front door.

Frank hurried to catch up, fumbling for the keys. "It was built about two years ago by a rich retired banker who lived here with his wife until one night back in June when he jumped out of bed screaming, ran out of the bedroom and fell down the stairs – broke his damn neck I heard!"

"Anyway, the wife just wants to get rid of the place now, says it's cursed or something – just a bunch of nonsense if you ask me though. The old guy was probably half in the bag when it happened!" Frank laughed, "But you'll probably hear a hundred different stories from the locals – some say it's a former Indian burial ground, others claim that witches were burned nearby. Anyway, I can assure you it's nothing but a load of crap!" he quickly added, worried that he had already let his mouth run on a bit too long.

Edgar laughed along with Frank. He was neither impressed nor deterred by any of these stories. He had faced down everything from angry teamsters to armed robbers while running his trucking company and was not about to be scared off by silly rumors and old wives tales.

So in less than a month's time, Edgar was able to gather all the required financial assets and ended up buying the house with his wife Janet and their two young daughters Maggie and Elizabeth. They would all live quite happily for the next 14 years or so with no apparent effects from the 'curse' that affected some of the earlier residents. However, during this time, the oldest daughter, Maggie, who had always been pleasant and cheerful, slowly grew sullen and defiant, seemingly hating everything and everyone.

While attending high school, she had been disciplined for everything from fighting with other students to spitting at a teacher until she was finally expelled for setting a fire in the school auditorium.

After being expelled, she would occasionally try, half-heartedly at best, to get a job, but no one seemed interested in a foul mouthed, anti-social high school dropout. She spent most of her time hanging around downtown and getting into trouble which just added to her bitterness and anger.

Several years later, at the age of 22, Margaret was as angry and repulsive as ever. Her inner ugliness had broken through to the surface and was now reflected in her appearance as well – from her thick yellow toenails to her rotten, crooked teeth which were stained brown from years of chewing tobacco. She was easily the ugliest woman in town and quite possibly the ugliest woman in the county.

Her twenty-one year old sister Elizabeth on the other hand was a cheerful, outgoing young woman whose beauty was in its prime. Petite, with blonde hair and blue eyes, her sunny disposition and dazzling smile made her well liked by nearly everyone she encountered – especially the area's young men. Although she was not very bright, she was kind and considerate – her only real flaw was her overly trusting nature.

What she lacked in wit, Elizabeth made up for with kindness and compassion. She frequently volunteered at the local nursery school, delivered meals to the elderly and worked at a homeless shelter on weekends.

As much as she resented her sister's good fortune, Margaret left her in peace and the two girls lived a relatively normal family life, at least from the outside. That is, until one summer evening when they received the news that both of their parents had died in a tragic car accident.

It was around eight o'clock on a cold, damp and dreary Friday evening. Edgar and his wife Doris were discussing food, or more specifically, restaurants. It had been their Friday night ritual for quite some time, even before they were ever married.

Tonight they decided to visit a familiar little café in a nearby town named Charlie's. It was a restaurant they both frequented regularly. Doris liked the friendly atmosphere, in the converted century old home and Edgar enjoyed the seafood which reminded him of his boyhood spent in rural New England.

They hopped into Edgar's self described "pride and joy," a 1970 Cadillac Coupe DeVille. After Edgar adjusted the radio and Doris checked her makeup one last time – they made their way down the long driveway and out onto the street.

About a mile down the road, Ed made a right turn onto a long narrow country lane. It ran for almost a half mile, straight as an arrow, until it bent abruptly to the left at an almost 90 degree angle. Though narrow, the road was mostly flat and smooth, with a slight rise just before the bend, where it crossed over a drainage ditch.

As they rolled along admiring the huge Maple trees that grew in abundance here, Edgar slowly but steadily pressed down on the accelerator. Soon he was over the posted speed limit of 25 – then 30, 35, 40, 50…

Doris looked over at Edgar and smiled. She knew what was coming as soon as Edgar made the turn onto this road. This was their secret guilty pleasure, to speed down this long, straight road until they hit the bump near the end, sending the car slightly airborne for several euphoric moments before landing – the closest thing to a roller coaster within 50 miles.

This time was no different. With practiced self-confidence, Ed brought the 4-ton machine up to 60 mph then released the accelerator as he reached the crest of the hill. The car flew through the air as Ed prepared for the hard braking and sharp left turn that he would have to execute to complete his little trick.

"Wheeee!" his wife cried out in glee, raising her arms as if she were on a carnival ride.

Edgar smiled widely, sharing her exhilaration, but as his foot hit the brake pedal he heard a faint pop and felt the pedal go straight to the floor with no resistance at all.

Edgar went cold inside – his wife looked straight ahead, still smiling, she didn't know she was about to die and Edgar had no time to tell her.

He wrestled frantically at the wheel in the split second before his imminent death, but his efforts were all in vain. With tires squealing, the careening car slid off the pavement and slammed head-on into one of the largest maple trees on the road.

The impact, which crumpled the front end of the car like an accordion, drove the steering column directly through Edgar's chest, crushing his ribs and snapping his spine as it burst though, leaving behind a grotesque mass of bloody, twisted metal and shattered bone.

His wife, Doris who was not wearing her seatbelt at the time, was launched through the windshield as if shot from a catapult. She struck the tree with enough force to snap her neck and shatter her skull.

Thankfully, both died painlessly.

A few minutes later a local resident, who was out walking his dog, came upon the gruesome scene and hurried home to call the police – after stopping briefly to vomit in the bushes.

After the coroner had removed the bodies and the police were putting their finishing touches on the accident report, a tow truck arrived to remove the wreckage. As the operator hooked the lift to the front end of the vehicle and began raising it, an observant detective named Chief Ken O'Connor noticed a stream of red brake fluid spurting from a dangling line. O'Connor, acting on a hunch, quickly ordered the tow truck operator to stop. He crouched down on the balls of his feet to get a better view of what had drawn his interest. After O'Connor had finished examining the line, he turned to his partner, detective Smith and said "This was no ordinary accident, I believe this was intentional." He held forth the cleanly severed brake line to Smith who nodded in agreement.

As they collected and packaged the final bits of evidence, O'Connor gave the okay to the tow truck driver to continue preparing the vehicle for towing. He and his partner now had the difficult task of breaking the news to the deceased couple's two daughters.

Maggie, if she felt any sorrow at all, managed to hide it well. Elizabeth on the other hand was devastated by the loss of her dear parents. Even more so when it became apparent that the car had been tampered with.

Chief O'Connor, who had been a good friend of Edgar Strain, had taken a personal interest in the case. His suspicions immediately fell upon Margaret, who was already well known in the community as a cruel and vindictive troublemaker. He believed that murder would simply be a minor step up for her.

So the next morning, O'Connor and detective Smith arrived at the Strain house to begin a rather uncomfortable interview with the two sisters whom the officers jokingly referred to as the Angel and the Troll.

As Chief O'Connor and detective Smith began their questioning, they brought up topics such as: Who worked on the car last? Was it in a mechanic's shop? If so whose? Did Edgar do his own automotive repair?

It appeared that Elizabeth was almost about to say something to that last question, when Margaret blurted out "Oh yea, dad did most of the work on the car himself. Why, was there a problem?"

O'Connor responded "Well yes actually. We believe that one of the brake lines was cut and that your parents were murdered."

Out of nowhere Margaret proclaimed "Well don't look at me! I don't even know what a brake line looks like, nor would I know how or where to cut one! In case you men haven't noticed, I am a woman and I'm not very knowledgeable about those types of things."

As Chief O'Connor peered at her suspiciously over his notebook, he noticed a small pinkish red stain on the front of her coveralls. At first glance it could have been anything from paint, to blood, or maybe even brake fluid. He questioned her about it and was met with "Oh that? It's probably just a tobacco stain. You see gentlemen, I prefer chewing tobacco rather than smoking it. Its probably just some spit that didn't make it past my clothes. You can ask Elizabeth, I've been working in the house and haven't been outside for the last 24 hours.

Chief O'Connor looked at Elizabeth and asked "Is this true?"

Elizabeth nodded her head in agreement. Tears were welling up in her eyes now which gradually began to flow down her cheeks. She asked Chief O'Connor, "Did they suffer?

"Excuse me?" responded O'Connor.

"Our parents, did they suffer? Were they in pain?"

O'Connor, in a feeble attempt to provide some level of comfort, put his arm around her and said "No. They were both killed instantly on impact."

After another half-hour of interviewing both women, the

officers were convinced that Margaret was somehow respon-
sible for her parent's death but they were unable to shake her
story and finally got up to leave.

"If you can think of anything that might help, don't hesitate to give us a call," said Smith.

"I certainly will officer, and thank you so much for your
hard work." Elizabeth said, smiling sincerely.

Margaret then led the officers to the front door.

As he walked through the door and onto the front porch,
Chief O'Connor turned and added, "Well thank you for your
time ma'am, and if you…"

"Blow it out your ass, pig." snarled Maggie, spitting a
stream of tobacco juice in his direction as she slammed the
door shut.

The two stunned police officers looked at each other in
silence for a moment.

"Someone should put a bullet in that thing's head one
day." muttered O'Connor.

"It would have to be a silver bullet to hurt that beast."
laughed Smith as they composed themselves and climbed
into their squad car to leave.

Despite their suspicions, the police could find no evidence
that directly implicated Margaret, nor anyone else for that
matter. The case was eventually closed and the sisters were
able to collect the considerable proceeds from their parent's
insurance policies which Maggie promptly placed into a
joint account – for safety's sake, as she told Elizabeth.

Elizabeth used some of her money to rent an apartment
downtown where she would be closer to the local churches,
schools, and the Salvation Army office – all the places where
she worked as a volunteer.

She loved her little town along with its residents and
would spend many hours running errands or just walking
around chatting with the locals. On many of her trips, she
would run into a young gentleman by the name of Joseph

Ryan – by accident she assumed.

Joe was a handsome young man of twenty-three who worked at the local hardware store where he secretly hoped to save enough money to enroll into a good college with the eventual goal of becoming a lawyer.

The first time he saw Elizabeth, he thought that she was the most beautiful woman in the world and vowed that some-day she would be his wife.

He carefully arranged to run into her at various spots around town, always offering to buy her a cup of coffee or a slice of blueberry pie at the diner. These offers were usually accepted by Elizabeth since she was smitten by the hand-some young man as well. They would talk and laugh, enjoy-ing each other's company until Elizabeth would regretfully excuse herself to continue her errands, while Joe began plan-ning his next ambush.

Soon the two were dating, and having a wonderful time together. A picture perfect couple people would think – it seemed like they were made for each other.

But not everyone agreed with that thought. Seeing the two young lovers together annoyed Margaret greatly. She had long ago given up on the notion of true love, hand-some princes and the rest of that romantic nonsense. Seeing her sister glowing with love and joy just angered her even more. Everything seemed to come so easily for Elizabeth she thought. People tended to dote on that cute little blonde as if she were some kind of princess while they look at me as if I were standing in a pile of crap! Well they can all go to Hell for all I care!

Margaret's hatred of her sister grew day by day until one fateful afternoon when Elizabeth stopped in for a visit. She rushed into the kitchen and exclaimed breathlessly, "Oh Maggie you won't believe this. Joe asked me to marry him and … we're engaged!"

There was a moment of silence that seemed to drag on

for minutes. When Margaret's response finally came it rang quite hollow; "Well then, if that's what you want... I hope you're happy."

Elizabeth thought the reply was somewhat unusual, but in her excitement and joy she wasn't gong to dwell on it. "Oh sis, I'm, so excited, I've never planned a wedding before, where do we start?" she asked.

"There's no rush, why don't you come back tomorrow and we'll go up to the attic and see if we can find mom's old wedding dress – I think she would have wanted you to wear it."

"Oh, what a wonderful idea!" exclaimed Elizabeth, "I just can't believe this is happening, it's like a dream come true!"

"Yes... yes it is" Maggie replied, her voice flat and emotionless, "Well, it's getting late – you run along now, I need to take a drive into town this evening. There are some things I've been meaning to pick up."

Joe Ryan was busily working at the hardware store that same afternoon, whistling a somewhat tuneless but happy melody as he went about his chores. He had just finished tidying up the display of towels and bed linens when the door chime sounded indicating the arrival of a new customer. He looked up hopefully but immediately his heart began to sink. Margaret Strain had just walked in, wearing her usual filthy denim overalls along with her big clunky work boots. The only difference in her otherwise typical appearance was that this morning, she had chosen to cover her normally greasy brown hair – which was falling out in big uneven patches – with a new baseball cap which she had probably just shoplifted from the local five and dime store.

She stomped over to the fasteners section and picked out some assorted u-bolts, a length of heavy chain and a heavy rubber mallet. Joe put on his best smile as she approached the checkout counter, "Good morning Maggie, and how are you doing today?" he said with as much false cheer as he could muster.

She dumped her selections on the counter and snarled "Where's your bathroom?"

"Uh . . . it's right back there . . . on the left" Joe replied uncomfortably. Margaret stalked off to the bathroom and slammed the door. She emerged about ten minutes later accompanied by a stench that made Joe's eyes water. Giving up on making small talk, he silently rang up her purchases as quickly as possible.

"That will be $2.95 please" he said as he accepted the crumpled five dollar bill that Maggie threw on the counter. He handed her the change and said, "Well, thank you Maggie, and give my best to Elizabeth."

Margaret was staring at the change in her hand, "What the hell is this?" she demanded in her usual belligerent tone, "I gave you a ten!"

Stunned, Joe started to say something but then thought better of it. He sighed in resignation – five dollars was a lot of money and it would have to come out of his pay – but he didn't want to take any chances on losing Elizabeth, so he simply opened up the register, noting that the $10 slot was empty, and handed Maggie a $5 bill.

"I'm sorry, I must have…" but Maggie snatched the bill from his hand and without a word, stomped off toward the door, pausing only to spit a wad of tobacco juice onto the neatly folded bath towel display near the front window.

She returned home, grabbed some of the tools from the garage and went upstairs to the attic where she busied herself for quite some time. When she finally returned downstairs, she grabbed a pen and sat down to write a short note – in uncharacteristically feminine handwriting – and addressed it to Joe Ryan.

Early the next day Elizabeth returned, still excited and anxious to try on her mother's dress. Dashing through the front door, she ran up to her sister and gave her a big hug which Maggie endured uncomfortably, until Elizabeth scurried off, practically running up the attic stairs.

Once upstairs, she began rummaging through the many boxes and chests, wondering where the dress might be. She was so absorbed in her search that she didn't hear Margaret softly climbing the attic stairs – or see her pick up the heavy rubber mallet which she raised above her head as she approached from behind.

Hours later, Elizabeth awoke on the attic floor with a throbbing pain in her scalp. She rubbed her eyes, trying to clear the blurred vision and then slowly stretched her limbs, stopping suddenly as she heard the sound of clanking metal. She looked down at her leg in horror. There was a steel shackle clamped around her left ankle which was attached to a heavy chain which in turn was bolted to the floor.

Elizabeth's eyes darted around the attic for something she could use to get herself out of this predicament but all the boxes, trunks and other accumulated belongings had been moved out of her reach. Shackled by the three foot long chain, she was unable to reach anything but the edge of the attic window – she was trapped!

"Maggie!" she called out, but there was no answer. Hearing the sound of a car engine, she moved as close to the window as she could. She was able to peer out just in time to see her sister pulling out of the driveway. Her car was packed with boxes and other items, and a large trunk had been strapped to its roof.

Elizabeth began to panic, "MAGGIE" she screamed, "Maggie please, Maggie…", but the car pulled onto the road and disappeared. Elizabeth continued to alternate between screaming and crying for the rest of the afternoon until she was too exhausted to do either.

It soon became obvious that her sister was gone for good, leaving her to die in the attic for some unknown reason. All the screaming in the world wouldn't save her now. The house was very well constructed with thick walls and tight window seals as well as being some distance from the lightly traveled road. There was little chance that she would ever be heard by anyone except for the few mice that inhabited the attic.

So as the days slowly crept by, the stifling attic became her prison. She had no food to eat nor barely any water to drink. If it weren't for the occasional passing thunderstorm and leaky roof, she would have died of thirst within the first few days. Instead, she managed to prolong her agony by lapping up the foul tasting water from a small puddle that formed on the attic floor.

As each day went by her misery increased. After nearly two weeks in captivity Elizabeth was near death. The former beauty had been reduced to mere skin and bones. The sores on her ankle, caused by chafing against the metal shackle, had become infected and gangrenous.

Her will to live had evaporated, along with her puddle of drinking water, until one afternoon when she heard a sound coming from the road in front of the house.

It was the faint sound of a young girl singing. At first, she thought she was delirious with fever, but as she listened closer, the singing continued, loud and clear and seemed to be getting closer! As she listened, the singing suddenly stopped and she heard the girl cry out in pain.

Too weak to scream, Elizabeth marshaled what little strength she had left and began to crawl toward the attic window until she reached the end of her chain. Desperate to escape, she tugged on it, heedless of the flesh being shredded off of her ankle, until her emaciated foot tore through the shackle, leaving bits of putrid flesh and bone clinging to the metal clasp. Nearly passing out from the pain, Elizabeth used her remaining strength to drag herself to the window and slowly pulled her head up to the glass pane.

It was turning out to be a beautiful summer day. The air was warm with very little humidity and the skies were bright and sunny. A perfect day to go exploring thought Patricia Pickell as she rode her bike down a bumpy dirt road. Like many fourteen year olds, Patricia loved horses. When not at school or studying Latin – her favorite subject – she would likely be found at one of the nearby farms, riding and grooming the horses, cleaning their stalls and performing the countless other tasks required to keep the animals alive and healthy. But it was the hands-on work with the horses that she enjoyed most and she gladly gave up nearly all of her free time just to be near these majestic creatures.

Having already checked in at the regular farms near her house she had decided to widen her search for employment. She explored as far as her bicycle would take her, which on this day, would be Hurley Pond Road.

She rode along singing a happy tune, her eyes darting left and right, scouring the landscape for signs of a horse farm. Suddenly she saw movement out of the corner of her eye and being startled, lost control of her bicycle. She came crashing to the ground, her knee gashed and bleeding painfully, the dirt and stones from the gravel road grinding deep into her torn flesh. She daubed at the clotting blood with a handkerchief, removing most of the pebbles and dirt, but some of the tiny bits remained lodged in her flesh.

Once the bleeding had slowed and her tears had dried, she finally was able to pick her head up and immediately became aware of the house looming up in front of her. It was a rather large house, some might even call it a mansion. It had several smaller outbuildings and a sizeable barn. The property itself covered quite a large area with several open fields lined with tall oak trees and a fenced in pasture for livestock.

Patricia was somehow drawn to the clean but somewhat

severe lines of the structure. What might appear sinister to some, she found quite comforting. As she stared at the house she whispered, with surprising certainty in her voice, "This will be my home someday".

Then, shaking her head as if waking from a dream, Patricia brushed herself off and remounted her bike. As she prepared to pedal away, a ghostly image appeared in one of the attic windows. The figure seemed to claw at the glass, trying to catch the girl's attention.

Looking through the attic window Elizabeth saw young Patricia mounting her bicycle and tried to scream but only weak croaking sounds came out. Not having enough strength to break the glass, she clawed desperately at the windowsill until trickles of blood dripped from her torn fingernails. This was her last chance to escape from the attic alive.

But the girl on the bike never turned back and as she disappeared down the road, Elizabeth Strain crumpled to the attic floor. She no longer had the strength nor the will to go on. The only thought on her mind as she died was "Why?"

Meanwhile, Joe Ryan was acting like a man on a mission. He had been counting down the minutes until five o'clock arrived, and at the top of the hour, he practically ran out of the store.

His boss, Paul Miller called after him, "Hey Joe, where you going so fast? Off to see your woman?"

"Yeah, she's finally back from wherever the hell she's

been all this time." he answered as he dashed out the door.

A week ago, he had received a note, apparently signed by Elizabeth, saying that the two sisters would be away for two weeks on "emergency family business." Although he thought it strange that she would write a note instead of talking to him directly, he went about his business as usual and waited patiently for his fiancee to return.

Driving his old pickup truck at breakneck speed, he soon arrived at Elizabeth's apartment but was immediately disappointed – the piled up newspapers showed that Elizabeth had not yet returned. Not wanting to wait, he decided to drive over to her sister Maggie's house to see if they had stopped there first. He felt it would be worth the discomfort of having to talk to Maggie if he could see Elizabeth that much sooner.

However, as soon as he arrived at the house, he knew something was wrong. Maggie's car was not in the driveway, and when he looked in the window he saw boxes and belongings strewn about the normally neat household. With his fears rising, he decided to drive over to a neighbor's house to call the police.

As he waited, he thought about Maggie – everyone knew she was mean and obnoxious, but was there something else? Although he couldn't quite put his finger on it, he felt there was something truly dangerous about her the moment they met. Her air of detachment and almost total lack of emotion was such a bizarre contrast to her sister who was always friendly and outgoing.

But what bothered him most was the way Maggie looked at Elizabeth. He could see the raw hatred in her eyes and once even mentioned it to Elizabeth, but her cheerful good nature blinded her to many of the evils in the world and she refused to believe that her sister would ever think ill of her.

Joe put aside his thoughts as the police car arrived. He explained the circumstances to the officer who agreed to break open the front door and investigate, warning Joe to wait outside.

As soon as the officers entered the house they performed a quick search of the ground floor and then headed upstairs. Joe waited nervously in the living room until he heard one of the officers gasp. He quickly bounded up the stairs to the attic where he saw one of the cops trying to find a pulse on a very emaciated Elizabeth. The police officer turned to Joe and said "She must have passed away a few hours ago or less." Joe's eyes began to pool with tears. He dropped slowly to his knees and grabbed the heavy chain and u-bolt. He turned to the police officer and said "I sold these to her sister Maggie. I supplied her prison, I supplied her demise." The police officer stood up and tried to give Joe some comfort.

Several minutes later another police car arrived, followed by an ambulance and finally, the coroner's van.

Upstairs in the attic, the coroner stood over the body of Elizabeth Strain. He was shocked to discover that despite the almost skeletal remains, the victim had been dead mere hours. He estimated the time of her death to be approximately three o'clock that afternoon. The cause – homicide.

On a warm September evening, barely a month after the Strain murder, Chief O'Connor again found himself on Hurley Pond Road. He watched as the local volunteer firefighters vainly attempted to douse the raging flames that had engulfed the Strain house. Despite their best efforts, the once imposing structure was now reduced to a crackling pile of embers.

As Fire Chief Nolan poked around the smoldering ruins, he muttered "It doesn't look like arson to me, probably just lightning."

O'Connor looked up at the clear, calm evening sky but said nothing. He didn't really want to know what happened as long as the cursed house was gone. Maybe now the town could get back to normal.

With Maggie Strain having disappeared and no known next of kin, the Strain property reverted to the state and was soon put up for sale.

CHAPTER TWO

DARK WATERS

Once again the local realtor, Frank Sampson, found himself driving a prospective client over to the site of the former Hurley Pond Road house. Unlike the trip five years ago, he was not his usual jovial self. He had watched the deterioration of the Strain family over the years and no longer laughed at the tales of evil, hauntings and other supernatural events which had become synonymous with the estate.

His client that day was a young engineer by the name of Chett Baxter who, like Edgar Strain, immediately fell in love with the scenic property.

He was not at all deterred by the burned out ruins of the original residence, some of which still remained, for he intended to construct a new mansion of his own design. Something constructed from the ground up to accommodate his oversized, six foot, seven inch frame.

Chett fully intended for this to be his dream home. "I will live the rest of my life here and I will probably die here." he thought wistfully, picturing himself as an old man sitting on the front porch with dozens of grandchildren playing in the fields.

He poured over the old blueprints which he'd been collecting for a number of years; picking and choosing portions of his favorite renderings from a number of previously built homes. A master bedroom here, a mahogany library there, a wine cellar in the basement, and on and on he went, designing his dream home on paper.

When construction finally began, it only took three short months and the results were better than expected. Using all of his design and engineering skills he created a masterpiece of practical beauty with vaulted ceilings and oversized doorways which were perfectly proportioned to the large rooms resulting in a majestic feeling of openness and light. The walls were covered with rich wood paneling topped by intricately molded plaster ceilings. The floors were built out of one inch thick oaken planks, which were stained and polished to a mirror-like finish. Additional elaborate trimming details consisted of limestone flooring, bluestone patios, and copper gutters topped off with a slate roof. The perfect marriage of comfort and elegance.

Downstairs you would find the formal living room, a large dinning room featuring a beautiful brick fireplace, a wood paneled den with exotic cork flooring, a large modern kitchen and an expansive family room.

Chett had spared no expense in building this house. His combinations of the finest materials and the latest luxury features created a dwelling that bore the unmistakable mark of a master craftsman.

In this impressive house, Chett Baxter and his wife Helen would continue raising their three children. Steven who was the oldest at twenty-two, Peter, the middle child at age twenty and Donna the youngest at eighteen.

Steven was Chett's pride and joy. Tall and lean like his father, he was a champion diver and captain of the swim team at Rutgers University where he was entering his senior year. Steven had brains as well as athletic ability and was preparing to graduate with an engineering degree, much to the delight of his father.

Chett's daughter Donna was also a great source of happiness for him. Slim and pretty, she had a bubbly personality and smile to match which could light up any room. A recent high school graduate, Donna had also been accepted at Rutgers University, making her the first Baxter woman to attend college.

The middle child Peter, however was a bit of a disappointment for Chett. The ostentatious twenty year old had been quite a handful ever since he was a youngster. Though smart and talented, he never seemed to fully apply himself at school. He was adept however, at continually finding new ways to get himself into trouble for his involvement in a variety of pranks, jokes and petty vandalism. He finally ended up being expelled from high school for driving a car onto the baseball field during a game.

After his expulsion he decided to leave home and spend his time drifting around the area working as a mechanic whenever he needed money. He remained in contact with his family, making regular visits to his parent's house for laundry and home cooking.

Still, Chett had a soft spot in his heart for Peter; he was a smart kid but lacked direction. Chett still had hopes that he would eventually figure out what he wanted out of life and put his talents to good use.

The Baxter family lived happily in their new house for several months before their comfortable world began to crumble.

Enjoying his last few days at home during the summer break, Steven was practicing diving at the local reservoir one hot afternoon. Having grown up there, he knew every inch of the area, above and below the water level. However, as he gracefully leapt from the edge of a small cliff, he didn't notice the submerged tangle of tree trunks and roots that were hidden just out of sight in the murky water below.

He hit the water perfectly, with hardly a ripple to show that he was ever there, but as he angled back up toward the surface, something went horribly wrong. His legs became entangled in the twisted branches and vines of the submerged trees. He tried with all his might to extricate himself from its deadly grip, but his efforts were in vain. Soon his lungs began to fill with water and the thrashing of his arms and legs slowed until they, like his heart, became still.

It was weeks before Steven's bloated body was discovered and pulled from the dark waters; his sightless eyes still open wide in a mask of fear and surprise.

Chett and Helen were devastated when they heard the news, but it was Donna who took Steven's death the hardest.

Always cheerful and outgoing, she had recently joined up with the new 'hippie' movement which was sweeping the nation and had taken to wandering the streets with her shaggy friends, dancing, smiling and flashing peace signs at everyone they saw.

But soon after Steven's death she had become quiet and withdrawn, no longer spending time at the park or the other hippie hangouts. Instead, she had acquired a new set of friends, just as hairy and dirty as the hippies but far more dangerous.

She spent most of her time downtown, only coming home to sleep – or try to. Since Steven's death, her nights were restless and filled with nightmares in which she heard voices; actually a single voice, deep and menacing that echoed in her mind. The words were mostly unintelligible, but their threatening tone left little doubt as to the speaker's intentions.

Seeking relief from her persistent nightmares, Donna began to experiment with alcohol and drugs, until, in one of her darker hours, she found a friend in heroin. With the first plunge of the needle, her fears, then all of her cares, drifted away. The lethargy, vomiting and collapsed veins were a small price to pay for such comfort.

Helen noticed the change in her daughter right away. "Chett, I'm worried about Donna and those new friends of hers, we don't know anything about them – except that they have long hair and smell bad!"

"I know", replied Chett, "Ever since Steven's death she's…"

"Ever since moving to this house, you mean!" interrupted Helen.

"Oh please, not that again" Chett said wearily. He had heard her complaints a hundred times or more over the past year that they had been living there.

"There's something creepy about this place, I just don't feel comfortable here." Helen would say, looking around her shoulder as if something in the woodwork was about to jump out at her.

Chett took it personally of course – it was his design and he had built much of it with his own hands. Whenever Helen brought up the subject – and it was often – Chett would end up trying to calm his temper with liquor, which only made matters worse.

Over the next few weeks, they grew further and further apart, with Chett spending most of his evenings in the den, sipping fine imported brandy, wondering how things had gotten so bad since – well, since building and moving into this house.

It was during one of these evenings that his thoughts were interrupted by the sounds of whispering voices. He would try to listen more intently but could only make out the sounds of leaves rustling in the wind. Shrugging it off, he picked up a book and began to read. Again he was stopped by the faint sounds of voices and again he would listen closely, but there was only the sound of the wind. Episodes like this would happen nearly every night. The maddening sound of barely audible voices, whispering and laughing at him from afar.

Chett found that brandy and scotch could provide fast,

temporary relief from all of his problems. He would consume several large glasses every night before unsteadily making his way up the stairs to bed.

Finally, after several weeks, the voices gradually diminished as did Chett's drinking. As a consequence, his fights with Helen became less frequent and they began to resume their formerly happy relationship.

On one warm sunny afternoon Chett and Helen decided to go shopping together. Helen wanted to pick up a new dress for Donna, hoping that the surprise gift might pick her up from the depression that she had fallen into lately.

After a pleasant afternoon of shopping together like the old days, Chett and Helen returned home. Chett retired to the family room and turned on the TV while Helen unwrapped the new dress along with a new pair of shoes that they had purchased for Donna.

Running upstairs to Donna's room Helen called out gaily, "Donna honey, you know that dress you liked at the mall…" but as she entered Donna's room, her words turned into a scream.

Her only daughter was propped up in the corner, staring straight ahead. Her gray, pale skin only highlighted the dark ugly circles under her unseeing eyes. The rubber tube was still wrapped around Donna's arm, the needle still hanging from a scarred blue vein. Her mother screamed again, this time loud enough to bring Chett running up the stairs.

As Chett entered the room the rubber tourniquet slipped and a gush of dark, semi congealed blood spurted from Donna's ruptured vein, splattering the white linen curtains of her bedroom. Horrified, Chett turned away, unable to look at the gruesome spectacle of wasted flesh and clotted blood that was once his daughter.

CHAPTER THREE

Shadows in the Mist

Soon after Donna's overdose, Chett began to take an interest in the history of the house. He remembered the vague warnings from the realtor about the tragedies that had befallen some of the former tenants and decided to do a little investigative work on his own. He would occasionally spend his afternoons at the local diner talking to patrons who were more than happy to relate stories about the so called "Evil House" on Hurley Pond Road. He also made the occasional visit to the town library in order to search through the newspaper archive section for articles related to the house. He was amazed and disturbed by the sheer number of incidents that apparently unfolded at the property. Chett soon amassed a folder stuffed to the brim with clippings and notes that went back over a hundred years, detailing a seemingly endless list of murders, suicides, tragic accidents and fires.

Though not a superstitious man by any means, Chett began to wonder if his dream home really was "possessed" as so many people believed. Being a logical and rational man, Chett was uncomfortable with the supernatural as a whole, and was unprepared to deal with the situation he found himself in. As a consequence, he soon fell back into his habit of drinking in the den each night.

At first, the alcohol provided some measure of relief, but soon the voices returned – this time louder and clearer than ever before. Some sounded like Steven, some sounded like Donna, but there was one voice in particular that he didn't recognize; a deep, dark, almost demonic voice that truly sent shivers up his spine.

Each night for the following three weeks at around nine o'clock, Chett was drawn to the den like a moth to a flame. Sometimes the voices would come, sometimes they wouldn't, but as always, there was a palpable tension in the air; a faint feeling of dread as he waited, knowing that something would soon be happening; something that would finally give him peace.

Finally, one night, just after nine o'clock, Chett walked into his den, settled down into his worn leather office chair which was always positioned neatly behind his desk and poured himself a small brandy. He began to reminisce about his children; the many happy times they had together when Steven and Donna were young. His thoughts strayed to his middle boy, Peter. Very much the rebel, Peter had caused his father unending aggravation over the years, but he was Chett's only living child at this point which proved to be some source of comfort.

Despite being the proverbial black sheep of the family, Peter was a very intelligent man. Unfortunately, his total lack of respect for authority had kept him from achieving his true potential in life while also creating several run-ins with local law enforcement.

Although he would stop in to see his mother and father once in a while, he had not paid a visit since Donna's funeral. Chett loved his son dearly, despite his weaknesses, and prayed that some angel would watch over him.

Having finished his first drink of the night, Chett opened the folder which he had labeled "Our House", and spread the contents around the desktop. He began to scan the various headlines.

"LOCAL GIRL DIES OF DRUG OVERDOSE"

"PROMISING YOUNG SWIMMER DROWNS IN RESERVOIR"

"HURLEY POND RESIDENCE DESTROYED BY FIRE"

"BIZARRE MURDER ON HURLEY POND ROAD"
"BOY DIES IN AUTO ACCIDENT ON HURLEY
POND ROAD"
"FIVE HORSES DIE IN RAGING BARN FIRE AT
HURLEY POND – POLICE INVESTIGATE"
Chett stopped to rub his eyes, then opened the bottom
drawer of his desk, reaching for a bottle of scotch and a new
glass. He poured himself an ample amount and took a sip,
savoring the rich aroma and admiring the amber color. After
a moment, he got up and walked over to one of the bookshelves that lined the walls. His fingers felt along the edge
of the mahogany until he pressed a latch which was all but
hidden in the decorative wooden molding of the bookcase.
A panel popped open to reveal a small hidden cabinet which
contained an object wrapped in an oily rag. Hesitantly, he
picked it up and returned to his desk.

He opened the rag and removed a Ruger .38 caliber revolver and placed it onto his desk. A gun lover since boyhood, Chett always enjoyed handling weapons and this one
was a real beauty. He had found it while rummaging around
in the burnt out ruins of the previous house. Admiring the
highly detailed French walnut grips, he began running the
rag over the blue steel barrel which was just a habit since the
gun was always kept in pristine condition.

Suddenly he heard a voice – Donna's voice. Shaken, he
picked up his glass of scotch and finished it in one gulp. As
he sat trying to calm himself, his eyes begin darting around
the room, finally coming to rest on Donna's photograph over
the mantle. She looked so young and innocent, a stark difference from his last image of her emaciated, drug ravaged
body. Suddenly, he heard Donna's voice; "Hi dad, it's me,
your little girl", "Do you still love me dad?"

Shocked and confused, Chett started to reply "Of course I
do honey…" only to be cut off by Donna's voice.

"Then Do it!" "Do it dad!" which she repeated over and

over.

Chett began to wonder if he was going crazy, nothing made sense. "Do what honey?" he asked, but all he heard was "Do it, do it dad!"

Shaking, he turned away to gaze out the window, but there, inches from the windowpane, he saw what appeared to be a ghostly vision of his son Steven. But it was not the Steven that he remembered. All he saw was the bloated and decaying body which was dragged from the dark waters of the reservoir where he had drowned. Steven opened his mouth in an apparent attempt to speak, but no words came forth; only tiny crayfish emerged which had been eating his organs from the inside. They rapidly crawled down his chin and fell away to the ground.

Horrified, Chett looked away. He angrily swept the newspaper clippings onto the floor when his attention was momentarily grabbed by the sight of the pistol in front of him. His trembling hands picked up the gun and without thinking, he checked the action and froze – Chett, meticulous in his care of the pistol, always kept it unloaded, but tonight there were six bullets in the cylinder.

Suddenly it all made sense to Chett. He felt a calm wash over him, as if the weight of the world had finally been removed from his shoulders. He slowly placed the pistol to his temple and quietly muttered "Screw it!" as he pulled the trigger. Chett did not hear the explosion nor did he feel the bullet that blew away most of his skull.

The wall to his left was covered with blood, brains, bone fragments and bits of unidentifiable tissue that oozed slowly towards the floor. His body gradually slumped over until the remains of his head hit the desk with a dull thud. Blood spurted from a torn artery and flowed over the edge of his desk where it dripped onto the scattered newspaper clippings and into the cork flooring below.

Hearing the shot, Helen came racing into the den, only

to stop suddenly as she caught the sight of her husband's lifeless body slumped over his desk. Frozen with shock, she stood there for a moment trying to comprehend the scene before her – they were going through some hard times but Chett was not the type of person to commit suicide. But there he was, revolver still clutched in his right hand.

Staring in confusion, she suddenly felt a jolt of raw terror as the body of her husband began to sit upright in its chair. As she backed away slowly towards the door, Chett's dripping visage seemed to look at her through its one remaining eye. Suddenly Chett raised his arm and fired the gun. The shot missed her by mere inches as Chett collapsed back onto the desk, his finger still twitching on the gun's trigger.

After Chett's funeral, Helen became a recluse, never telling anyone of the horrifying incident which occurred *after* Chett's death when his lifeless body somehow fired a gun at her.

She rarely ventured outside anymore, and soon began to hear the strange voices as well, both at night and during the day. She convinced herself that they were most likely being brought on by her extreme isolation.

Helen countered this by asking her son Peter if he would like to move in with her. Peter, being between apartment rentals at the time, agreed and moved his few belongings into his old room. He had recently taken up with a local motorcycle gang and spent most of his evenings with them acting as their club mechanic. But on one particular evening, he decided to stay home to keep his mother company. They had a pleasant dinner, enjoying the food and talking about happier times until the mood was suddenly interrupted by a loud crashing noise coming from upstairs in Donna's old bedroom.

Both of them jumped up and rushed to investigate. Her bedroom, which had been untouched since her tragic death, was now in disarray. The crash must have come from Donna's jewelry box which now lied smashed to pieces with the contents spilling out across the hardwood floor.

Peter attempted to explain away the odd occurrence by postulating that the box might have walked itself to the edge of the shelf over time until just a small vibration sent it crashing to the ground. Helen accepted this explanation gratefully, wanting desperately to believe that it was just a natural occurrence. They gathered the scattered earrings, necklaces and bracelets, and returned them neatly to their respective drawers.

Over coffee, Peter suggested to Helen that she might want to think about putting up one of her spare bedrooms for rent which would give her some much needed company along with an added sense of security whenever Peter was away.

Helen was very receptive to the idea and submitted an ad to the local newspaper the very next day. She and Peter agreed that Donna's room was probably best suited for rental purposes and spent some tearful moments packing up her old belongings. After cleaning out the room, Helen began to feel better about her situation and hoped that her mourning process might finally be coming to a close.

Helen's ad was quickly answered by a local woman named Barbara White. Barbara's physical and mental strength as well as her kind, welcoming personality immediately impressed Helen. Since she didn't really need the extra income, she offered the room at a rate of only fifteen dollars a week, to which Barbara readily accepted and moved her belongings in immediately.

With Barbara now living in the house, Helen's nights became quiet and peaceful. The two quickly became friends and Helen confided in Barbara about the many tragedies that had befallen her household. After a few of these much needed catharsis, Helen began to feel her sorrow and depression lift even further.

Barbara rapidly adjusted to her new surroundings and began taking regular walks along the expansive property. One moonlit autumn night, while walking near the center of the horse corral she noticed a spot where the temperature was unusually cold, almost to the point of freezing. She crouched down low, holding her hand inches above the ground until she was able to feel a steady stream of frigid air seemingly rising straight out of the earth.

Suddenly an icy chill shot through her spine – she rose quickly as she noticed a thick fog like mist emanating from the woods and slowly moving towards her from across the field,. Barbara calmly but briskly made her way back to the house, trying to remain calm until she reached the side door. Before entering, she glanced over her shoulder at the odd mist that had seemingly appeared out of nowhere. It had continued it's approach at a more rapid pace than before and looked as if it might engulf her at any moment. She quickly yanked open the door, stepped inside and deadbolted it behind her. Barbara flicked on the kitchen light and pulled the curtains back slightly to peer into the misty darkness. Maybe it was just the moonlight playing tricks in the shadows but she thought she saw what appeared to be the silhouette of a tall dark figure standing in the middle of the corral where she had just retreated from. Barbara quickly turned off the kitchen light to get a better view but instead was met with bright lights piercing through the thick fog along the road. She sighed with relief as Helen's car appeared through the mist.

Barbara decided to let Helen settle in for a bit before relating her experience. After an hour or so had passed, Barbara went downstairs to the kitchen, casually made herself a cup of tea and then continued on to the den where she found Helen propped up in a comfy chair reading a tattered copy of *The Bell Jar*. She told her what had occurred earlier that evening and even laughed at herself a few times over how silly it all must have sounded. Although somewhat spooked by the story, Helen told Barbara that it often gets foggy in the fields around here and that the wind currents over a nearby lake sometimes brought unusually cool breezes – although it did seem to happen a little more frequently since Chett's death. Finally the two agreed that sometimes things were just a "little weird" at this house and began to laugh.

For the next several months, events at the house were quiet until strange things gradually began to happen again. At first the incidents were small – lights going on and off unexpectedly, the dining room chandelier going from dim to bright, spinning and shaking until it came to a dead stop and reverted to its normal settings.

Then in February, the strangeness began to escalate once again. It was a dark and dreary afternoon and the sky was full of heavy, low hanging clouds that seemed to be threatening snow at any minute. Helen had decided to venture out to do some mid-winter food shopping, while Barbara stayed behind to clean and straighten up the house.

She began in her room by dusting the armoire and credenza; getting rid of all the old bills and empty nail polish bottles; and throwing any unread magazines and miscellaneous junk into a cardboard box. She then temporarily rearranged her bedroom furniture to the opposite side of the room and headed off to retrieve the house vacuum cleaner from the hall closet. When she returned, she saw that her remaining nail polish bottles had been rearranged to form the shape of an inverted crucifix. Next to the crucifix, an open bottle now laid on its side with red polish spilling out onto the tabletop. Nearby was the small applicator brush which had apparently been used to write a threatening message on the wall in front of her – "LEAVE HERE NOW!!!"

Barbara panicked. She quickly decided that she had had enough and her only thought was to get as far away from the house as possible. She quickly grabbed her overcoat and reached for the bedroom door, but found it seemingly locked from the outside. Petrified, and knowing full well that there were no outside locks on any of the bedroom doors, she stood motionless, contemplating her next move. Then a voice behind her began to speak softly. "Barbara, would you like to get high with me?" Barbara quickly scanned the room. There in the corner, sitting at her makeup table was a young girl with an ashen complexion and dark circles under her eyes – eyes whose pupils had turned almost white. As the harrowing figure began to rise, Barbara noticed a tourniquet wrapped around her left arm and a syringe in her right hand. The figure waved the needle mockingly at Barbara then plunged it deep into her own arm. After emptying the syringe, the figure suddenly and rapidly approached Barbara. Barbara backed away instinctively but tripped over the vacuum cleaner landing face up on the bed, her eyes still fixed on the impossible vision standing in front of her. The spectre, moved closer still, positioning itself within inches of Barbara's face and said in an unnaturally deep voice: "Get the hell out of my room, and get the hell out of my house!" With these words echoing, in Barbara's ears, the tormented figure disappeared and the bedroom door popped back open.

In a blind panic, Barbara bolted out of the room, down the stairs and out the back door, not even bothering to close it behind her. She jumped into her car and drove away with the tires squealing.

The following afternoon, Barbara reluctantly returned to the house along with her brother Phil to help collect her belongings. Helen didn't appear to be home at the time, so Barbara and Phil agreed to spend as little time inside the house as possible. After only an hour of packing, Phil's pickup truck was filled and ready to go. Happy to be back in the safety of the truck, Barbara gave one final glance back towards the house as they pulled out of the driveway. Looking up at the room that she had occupied until last night, she saw what appeared to be the ghostly figure of a young girl smiling back at them, waving goodbye.

Barbara welcomed the opportunity to finally be able to spend a nice, quiet, uneventful night, free from any supernatural interruptions at her brother's house which was located just a few miles away.

She awoke late the next morning, feeling reasonably refreshed from a good night's sleep and a bit braver than she had felt over the past couple of days. Against better reasoning, she decided to drive back to the house after lunch during the brightest hours of the day to relate the story to Helen in order to let her know of her concern for her safety.

Upon arriving back at the residence Barbara again found herself second guessing the previous day's events as she stared up at the not so threatening looking house in the full light of the afternoon sun. She walked up to the front door, entered the house and quickly found Helen downstairs in the laundry room.

"Where have you been?" exclaimed a slightly surprised sounding Helen.

"Well actually, that's what I wanted to talk to you about.

Last night I had a particularly frightening episode and I've decided to move out – permanently."

Helen listened intently to Barbara's story from the previous night and after hearing the description of the girl in the window, she realized that it had to be an apparition of her deceased daughter, Donna. Helen became quite frightened upon hearing the story and begged Barbara to move back in.

"Not a chance." Barbara replied. "I don't even like sitting here. There just seems to be something horribly wrong with this place and I suggest you leave, the sooner the better. Even right now if possible."

"Where would I go?" asked Helen.

"Stay with your mother or get a hotel room, but you've got to get out of this place," replied Barbara. "You can send a mover for your belongings, or put the whole thing up for sale – but for God's sake, you must leave!"

Hearing the urgency in Barbara's voice made Helen quite frightened and she quickly decided that she'd better go upstairs and at least pack a suitcase.

Barbara on the other hand wasn't so keen on helping her pack so she decided to wait for her in the comfort of her own car. Upon exiting the house, she quickly noticed the lengthening shadows and realized that they must have been talking for longer than expected. Darkness could come as early as four o'clock at this time of year. Clouds had started to fill the sky, blotting out the remaining sunlight which didn't add to Barbara's enjoyment of the afternoon.

Upstairs, Helen was busily packing her suitcase for a three or four day trip with clothes and other miscellaneous belongings when she heard a faint voice; barely audible at first

"Where are you going?" the voice whispered "You can't leave, you must stay with us… you belong with us."

Helen, not sure if she was imagining the voice, and not

planning to stick around to see if she could hear it again, closed her half-packed suitcase and made a run for her car.

She barely stayed on her feet as she dashed down the stairs, through the dining room and on towards the swinging door that separated it from the family room. But before she could reach the door, it flew open in front of her all by itself. Helen has no time to ponder this latest event and at this point her only instinct was survival.

She ran straight through the newly opened door, with her left arm outstretched in order to grab the knob of the large dutch door which led out onto the porch. But while the dinning room door had opened for her as if to hasten her exit, this one seemed to have a different agenda. Without being touched, the deadbolt slid shut, trapping Helen inside. Her fear was nearly overwhelming as she frantically tried to slide back the deadbolt, but even in her adrenalin-boosted state, she was unable to budge it. Finally in a fit of hysteria, she kicked blindly at the door, and with one lucky blow, the bottom half swung open. She quickly ducked through the opening and scrambled away as fast as she could, half running, half crawling until she reached the safety of her car.

Once inside, Helen heard a series of loud banging noises coming from within the house. Glancing out of her passenger side window, she saw the back door repeatedly opening wide and then slamming shut again. Terrified, she fumbled with the keys, eventually managing to slide the correct one into the ignition which fortunately, started the engine on the first try.

Helen threw the gearshift into reverse while stomping on the gas but for some reason the car refused to move. Over the whine of the engine, she began to hear loud banging noises on the car itself as if someone were outside, pounding and kicking it, but there was no one there. The pounding increased in fury until the car actually started to rock back and forth.

With her panic rapidly approaching the breaking point, she fumbled hysterically at the controls, and somehow managed to put the car in drive, when a sudden violent twist of the vehicle forced her head into the side window, momentarily dazing her. Certain that she was going to die, a stunned Helen finally got the car in reverse and quickly lurched backward with a spray of gravel, flying down the stone driveway and screeching to a halt as she reached the street. With her car still rocking wildly, Helen dropped the gearshift into drive and screamed down the road, speeding past Barbara.

Barbara noticed the odd rocking of Helen's car as it passed by. She knew that something had to be very wrong and quickly followed in pursuit. As both cars got about halfway down the road, Helen's car finally stopped rocking and began to handle normally again.

Barbara, assuming that the worst was now literally behind her, glanced nervously in the rearview mirror back towards the house from which they had just fled from and was confronted with a most unpleasant site. There on the backseat, sat a distorted, dark, misshapen silhouette of a figure looking back at her from the rearview mirror. Barbara hit the brakes in a panic; her car fishtailed and spun wildly, finally coming to rest in an empty field. Then, with a sudden rush of air, the rear window exploded into millions of fragments of flying glass – then all was still, except for the beating of Barbara's heart.

Even though she was shaking uncontrollably from the ordeal, she was able to put the car in gear and headed back out onto the road. About 200 yards ahead, she was able to catch up with Helen who she then followed to the next crossroad. There, Helen turned right, and Barbara turned left – the two would never see each other again.

Later, Helen ended up taking Barbara's advice and sent movers to the house to collect her belongings and put them in storage. She felt uncomfortable being around anything that came from the house and would rather just get rid of everything; even her own belongings. She contacted the local real estate agent to put the house up for sale, eager to leave this chapter of her life behind.

Helen went on to find a suitable home in the same town, albeit several miles away. She immediately knew that this was the perfect home for her. From the clean lines of the structure, to its cedar shake siding and white trim; all made it seem like a smaller version of the old house on Hurley Pond Road. But in this case, she would feel far more comfortable on this small half acre of land rather than the overgrown 15 ½ acres of the old estate.

Most importantly of course – there would be no ghosts, spirits, demons, or other things that go bump in the night. Although she lived only a few miles away, she would never set foot near the old house or even drive down Hurley Pond Road again. Her remaining years would be spent enjoying the tranquility of her new sanctuary.

CHAPTER FOUR

A New Beginning

Eleven more years passed and Patricia Pickell had long since forgotten about falling off of her bicycle in front of the house on Hurley Pond Road. It was now December 1st, 1970 and the young girl had gracefully transformed herself into a young woman, who was married to a handsome engineer by the name of Barry Fitzgerald. Together they were in the process of raising two children, a daughter, eight year old Coreen, and a very curious five year old – me, Darren Fitzgerald.

Growing up, my dad Barry was my hero. He was a tall man, like I would become – six foot, seven inches to be exact, and very intelligent. He was an extremely talented engineer, who often worked on classified government projects for a local defense contractor. At the time I always thought, or at least hoped, that he was some kind of spy working for the CIA.

As a family, we had many great times together, often visiting our nearby relatives as we were planning to do on this particularly cold and blustery December morning.

We were on our way to visit my Cousin Jimmy whose family lived along one of the many rural back roads of New Jersey. I always enjoyed visiting cousin Jimmy's house. There were plenty of open fields to play around in and numerous large trees to climb. Jimmy would always try to scare us by telling stories about the horrible Jersey Devil – "He lives in these parts you know." as he scanned the open fields fearfully. I of course, being slightly older, knew better – there was no such thing as goblins, ghosts or something called the Jersey Devil.

Anyway, we soon reached Jimmy's house when suddenly, instead of stopping at my cousin's, my dad pulled into the driveway of a nearby house and stopped. It was a large two-story building with dormored windows on a steeply pitched attic roof. I assumed that it was probably some friend of my parents and asked, "Who lives here?"

My father replied; "I don't know, let's find out", and started to open the car door.

"We do!" my mother accidentally blurted out, before clasping her hand to her mouth.

"Well, I guess the cat's out of the bag kids… come see your new home!" my father laughed.

But before the words were even out of his mouth, my sister Coreen and I were out of the car and racing up the slate steps to the back door. As soon as we reached the door, it swung open to reveal the smiling face of cousin Jimmy! Apparently his family thought that it would be nice to have a house warming party for their new neighbors.

As the grown-ups were all talking, laughing and hugging, saying how great each other looked, Jimmy and I quietly snuck off to go exploring outside.

As we stood on the back porch wondering what kind of trouble we should get into first, we noticed movement to our right. There in the water of an overgrown fishpond were several large goldfish circling around the murky brown water. Jimmy bent down to get a better look when I decided that it might be a good idea to push him in.

Moments later, as I was busy rolling around on the grass laughing uncontrollably, cousin Jimmy picked himself up and slowly rose to his feet in the middle of the frigid fishpond. His wet hair was matted to the side of his head and he had a slightly dazed look on his face. Holding his dripping arms outstretched, he sluggishly stepped out of the pond. At first it appeared as if he was going to cry, but upon seeing me locked in hysterical fits of laughter, he started laughing right along with me.

Our parents quickly arrived outside to see what was causing such a commotion. I distinctly remember my aunt Pat being quite angry with me. She thought that it was so cute dressing Jimmy in that ridiculous sailor suit but now the suit was not only wet, but muddy as well and most likely, ruined.

Aunt Pat, accompanied by my mother took Jimmy back to her house for a change of clothes as my sister and I, along with the rest of our cousins began exploring the interior of the house and the many rooms contained within. Fourteen rooms to be exact, from the strange smelling attic to the large finished basement which had a nearly ten foot ceiling and wine cellar.

Coreen, along with my cousins Tommy and Lisa joined my father, uncle and I as we went upstairs to explore the second floor. Suddenly Coreen stopped and whispered in my ear, "Doesn't it feel like we've been here before?"

At first I thought she was kidding, but the expression on her face showed that she was dead serious. I looked around at the polished floors, the detailed moldings around the doors, the layout of the rooms themselves and it all did look kind of familiar to me. Kind of like a dream that I may have had long ago but couldn't quite recall.

But Coreen, still with that frightened look on her face, went on to say "I feel like we've lived here before – in fact that's my room over there." as she quickly ran over to the doorway. Before opening it, Coreen turned to me, closed her eyes as if she was trying hard to remember and slowly said, "There are two windows opposite this door with yellow curtains with a floral print. The floor has brown wall-to-wall carpeting – but there is a stain on the edge near the windows. The closet is on the left – it's paneled in pine and there are some wooden hangers still on the clothes bar."

As she opened her eyes I noticed that they seemed to be focused miles away as if awaking from a dream. I was getting a little freaked out by now and we both held our breath as she opened the door and entered. Daylight streamed in from the two large windows opposite the door, casting flickering shadows that almost hid the stain on the brown wall-to-wall carpeting but it were there just the same. The closet door was open, revealing a spacious, paneled interior which was crossed by a metal clothes bar holding up four wooden hangers.

"All right" I said, "Nice joke Coreen, you were in here before with mom and dad weren't you?" She said nothing but when she turned toward me, her face was as white as a sheet. She reached out with a trembling hand to steady herself on the doorknob and looked as if she might faint. "Darren, I'm sacred." was all she could say.

Suddenly I too was scared, in fact terrified. I stumbled out of the room and wandered around aimlessly until I found myself in another bedroom. As I looked around, I felt another jolt of panic – I have been here before too! As I took a few deep breaths to try to calm my nerves, Coreen came back in. She took one look at my face and said quietly "We'd better get back to the others."

Trying hard to block out what had just occurred, we rejoined our father and uncle who were heading back downstairs. I was the last in line, and paused momentarily at the top of the staircase. Always one to experiment, I tried to calculate how many steps my Ben Cooper action figure would bounce if I tossed it down the stairs.

As I dug the rubber figurine out from the bottom of my pocket, I happened to notice movement out of the corner of my eye. I quickly turned to look but the hallway was silent and empty. Shrugging it off, I cocked my arm and prepared to release the figure until WHAM!, I was violently struck from behind. So hard in fact that the wind was knocked out of me. I must have flown over the first eight steps before crashing hard and rolling like a crumpled rag doll to the bottom of the staircase.

All the guests rushed over at once to see what had happened, "Are you all right?" my father said. "You'd better watch your step until you get used to the layout of the new house!"

I stood up and brushed myself off, still shaking from the invisible assault. "I didn't fall." I said, "I was pushed!"

But no one would believe such a tale from a five year old, "You were the last one down!" exclaimed my uncle. Then, smiling, he turned to my father and said, "Boys that age have such overactive imaginations and lots of pride; he just can't admit that he tripped!"

My dad laughed and said "Maybe God pushed you as payback for pushing your cousin Jimmy into the pond!"

My uncle smiled and added "A push for a push." Then everyone was laughing – except for my sister. She knew that I was telling the truth but said nothing. Neither of us would speak of this event again until several years had passed.

Despite the ominous beginning, we moved our belongings into the new house and settled in without further incident. In fact, for the next eight months or so we were a happy, peaceful family – that is until the middle of November.

A brisk November wind brought a chill to the air on an otherwise bright and sunny afternoon. My parents were going out shopping and had decided that Coreen was old enough to baby-sit for me. She was a mature nine year old, while I was a hyperactive and rambunctious five and a half year old. There was a brief discussion between my parents about the wisdom of this arrangement, but in the end, they trusted us enough to take a chance. Little did we know that no adult in the world would be able to deal with the events that were about to occur.

As my parents pulled out of the driveway, the sky itself began to change quickly, going from bright sunlight to a dark gray overcast as if to signal an approaching storm. The big house suddenly seemed to grow cold and the lights began to flicker slightly, giving off an eerie, surreal glow. It was as if we were on the set of some old black and white movie production, where everything seemed lifeless and grey.

Coreen decided to call her friend Debbie who lived down the block, while I ventured into an adjacent room to play. As my sister began chatting, I went through the swinging door that led into the dinning room where I settled down in front of the fireplace with my GI Joe action figures. After a few minutes, my attention became focused on the glow of the now dying flames in the oversized hearth. I stared hypnotically at the glowing red embers, until suddenly they began to radiate bright orange, which then ignited into yellow flames as if being fed by some unseen wind.

Instead of being warmed by the fireplace I felt a sudden chill – the hairs on the back of my neck stood straight up as the fireplace quickly became a raging inferno. Huge flames were shooting up the chimney, threatening to spill out onto the floor. I stood frozen in wonder and fear – I had never seen anything like this before. But then, as quickly as it had begun, the flames died down until only a few glowing red embers remained.

As I stood there shaking, trying to comprehend what I had just seen, I heard my sister's voice screaming "Darren, stop playing with the phone!" I quickly ran into the kitchen, but as I entered, I found Coreen standing motionless, holding the phone to her ear – her face a deathly shade of white. She was trembling and seemed unable to speak, her eyes displaying a look of fear that I had never seen before.

I moved closer and began to hear a voice emanating from

the receiver – a voice I had never heard before, but one that would haunt me forever: "Get off the phone, NOW!" it screamed.

Coreen managed to stutter "Who... who is this?" Again, the demonic voice shouted "GET OFF THE PHONE NOW!!!"

Without thinking, I grabbed a steak knife from one of the kitchen drawers. If there was something in our house trying to threaten us, I was going to kill it. I was either pretty brave or pretty foolish but I wasn't about to stand around contemplating my next move. I quickly ran upstairs to my sister's room where the other phone was located and as I neared the door, I heard the faint sound of someone dialing.

Holding the steak knife outstretched in front of me I entered the room fully prepared to do battle with the intruder. But as I opened the door, there was no one there – that's when I noticed the telephone on the bed with the receiver off the hook, as if someone had been using it.

Suddenly there was the return of the cold chill that I had experienced just minutes before, and for the first time in my young life, I felt true fear, bordering on terror.

I dropped the knife and quickly turned and ran back downstairs. As I slammed through the kitchen door I saw that Coreen was still holding the phone which she quickly dropped when she saw the expression on my face. She ran over to me and shouted "Let's get out of here!" as she grabbed my hand.

We made our way out the front door and continued our mad dash across the yard, past the pond and through the apple orchard all the way to Debbie's house.

Once there, we eagerly told our story to Debbie's mom who shook her head in disbelief and accused us of having overactive imaginations. She did however allow us to stay with her until our parents returned home. I sighed to myself – out of all the adults we had confided in, our mother seemed to be the only one who believed us.

Despite these events, or should I say because of them, my sister and I would enjoy a childhood of almost perfect serenity punctuated by rare moments of sheer terror. Our house seemed like the *Ozzie and Harriet* show from TV – dad was a very successful engineer and mom, was a stay-at-home housewife. As we approached our first Christmas in the new house, we felt, for the most part, that we were living in a Courier and Ives print.

We found the perfect Christmas tree on our own property, which we neatly set up next to the fireplace in the family room. There we would gather in the evenings, listening to Bing Crosby and Bob Hope while actually roasting chestnuts over the open fire. After all was said and done, our first Christmas in the new house would last in my mind forever.

The Hasbro Toy Company had added several new play sets to the G.I. Joe Adventure Team lineup and I found all of them under our tree on Christmas morning. First, there was the "Search for the Mummy's Tomb" set which came with a yellow six wheeled vehicle, pick axe, shovel, net, and of course, a mummy in its sarcophagus. This set alone, in addition to the seven new G.I. Joe figures, was enough to keep me occupied for days at a time.

I remember the second set was the "Search for the Stolen Idol" which was a two and a half foot long yellow helicopter with a winch, cargo net, and realistic looking gems contained within an Indian Idol.

The third set arrived later that day when my grandparents came by with two more G.I. Joes plus the "Training Center". This was a three foot tall orange tower with an attached drag line for G.I. Joe to slide down, along with a cave, searchlight, tent and a pretty cool looking rubber snake.

For the next several weeks I was in a world of adventure, and my parents loved it as much as I did. I would play with my stuff for hours on end, never bothering a soul – or at least that's what I thought.

Soon after the New Year we took the Christmas tree down and Coreen and I moved our toys upstairs to our respective bedrooms.

I quickly made an elaborate setup of G.I. Joe figures and action sets in my bedroom. Using all of my new equipment as well as some of my older figures and accessories I set the stage for a dramatic hostage rescue, with several of my older G.I. Joes acting as prisoners and a group of three commandos preparing to stage the rescue.

I placed Land Adventurer Joe as the driver of the six wheeled vehicle and Astronaut Joe on top of the orange training tower. Sea Adventurer Joe was positioned on the ground, ready to sneak into the prison camp to release the captives.

I was pretty impressed with the setup and wanted to share it with someone else so I took a walk over to my sister's room. Her door was open but as I looked inside I saw her standing still with her mouth open with a shocked expression on her face. Seeing me in the doorway she silently motioned to the floor in front of her. One of Coreen's presents that year was a huge chess set consisting of a black and white checkered rug about four feet square and two full sets of large plastic chess pieces, each about 10-12 inches tall.

My eyes followed her finger to the rug where a game seemed to be in progress – I noticed that several pieces had been moved from their starting positions. Then as I watched, one of the black knights moved two spaces up and one space to the left – all by itself.

I didn't know a whole lot about the rules of chess at the time, but my sister said that "it" seemed to be playing a game against itself. As we looked on in disbelief at the match unfolding in front of us, the pieces continued to make a series of logical moves, finally ending in checkmate for white.

When the pieces came to a stop and the game seemed to have ended, my sister turned to me, smiled and said with a reserved air of excitement, "How cool was that!"

I wasn't sure if what I had just witnessed was either cool or very, very scary so I quickly returned to my room to mull over the latest "event". Upon reaching my door I noticed that it was now closed. I was pretty sure that I had left it open, as I was planning to bring Coreen in to see my toy setup.

I was more than a little nervous after what had just happened, so I slowly opened my bedroom door, fully expecting the worst. Unfortunately, I wasn't disappointed. The first thing I noticed was movement on the floor near my G.I. Joes. Wait a minute, it *was* my G.I Joes. They were moving as if brought to life.

The six-wheeled vehicle, driven by Land Adventurer Joe was rolling slowly in front of the training tower while Astronaut Joe was sliding down the line from the training tower towards the floor. Then I noticed the coolest thing of all – the helicopter was hovering several feet in the air!

I stood silently in the doorway, awestruck by the supernatural display occurring right in front of me. It was as if my playtime fantasies had come to life except that the actions of the figures were not what I had originally planned. Astronaut Joe was supposed to slide down the line and knock down the prison door, releasing the hostages, but instead he began to attack the unarmed prisoners with his assault rifle. As he pointed his gun at the individual prisoners, the figures fell down and lied there motionless.

Meanwhile, the other three figures that I had set up as guards were apparently fighting with each other. I remember one strangling the other with his bare, plastic hands while a third figure stabbed him in the back repeatedly with his K-Bar knife.

Then I noticed something even more disturbing, Land Adventurer Joe who was sitting in the six-wheeled vehicle, reached for his miniature .45 caliber service pistol and slowly put it to his own temple. He paused for several seconds as I looked on in horror. Then his plastic head actually rolled off of his shoulders and fell to the floor while the rest of his body slumped over the steering wheel.

Still, I was more amazed than scared at this point and I finally gained the courage to fully open the door and enter the room. As soon as my foot crossed the threshold, the action abruptly stopped. The remaining figures ceased whatever action they were involved in and the helicopter fell to the floor with a loud crash. It was only then that I noticed that Sea Adventurer Joe was still in the same exact position from where I left it. For some reason, it was the only figure that hadn't moved at all.

Hearing the crash of my helicopter from down the hall, Coreen came rushing into my room, "What was that!" she exclaimed.

When I told her what had just happened she looked at me and said. "We'd better keep this between ourselves."

I quickly agreed, since no one would believe us anyway.

That July I found myself riding horses with my mother which was rare as I would much rather be riding my dirt bike. I had received a Honda 50cc Mini Trail for my 6th birthday and thus began my lifelong love of off road motor sports. But this day, my mother seemed insistent on wanting me to ride with her so without attitude and with a sincere smile on my face we began to ride our horses across the fields behind our house.

As the horse's hooves hit the slate of the walkway that led to our back door, my mother turned to me and said, "Look Darren, in the window."

There in the attic window was a ghostly image of a young woman smiling and apparently waving at us. My mother calmly said "Wave back dear."

As we began to wave the figure's smile disappeared and her lips began to move as if she were screaming. As I focused on the moving lips trying to understand what she was saying, the entire face began to fade.

I blinked my eyes but the image had vanished. There was only the window curtain hanging undisturbed as if nothing had happened.

My mother and I decided to ride all the way to the pond and back. During the entire trip I paid no attention to my surroundings. I hardly even noticed the beautiful tree lined path that we were riding on. All I could see in my mind was that ghostly face in the window.

As we returned home, all was quiet. We put the horses back in the stable, hung up their bridles, removed their saddles and placed them onto wooden saw-horses.

My mother and I went inside to fix a late lunch while I ran along upstairs to gather some toys to keep myself busy until the food was ready. As I traveled up the stairs, I glanced briefly into my sister's darkened room and stopped suddenly.

There on the bed was a girl who appeared to be crying. I quickly realized that this was not my sister who was currently across the street at my cousin's house.

A cold chill rose from within me standing the hairs straight on the back of my neck. As I backed away slowly, the figure leaped from the bed and stood facing me. Her face was pale gray with dark rings around the eyes. Her lips were a bloodless black. Then she spoke in a deep demonic voice, "Leave this house." Then she was gone and the room was once again quiet, empty and dark.

I ran down the stairs to tell my mother what had just occurred.

"That's it. I'll take care of this." she said, "There will be no more trouble, trust me." She told me to stay with her at all times as she quickly walked over to the phone to call my aunt to arrange for her to come over that evening at nine o'clock.

Soon after, Coreen returned from my cousin's house and my mother let her in on the latest event.

"What are we going to do?" Coreen asked nervously.

"Your aunt Cookie is going to be here right around nine o'clock tonight and I'll *show* you what we're going to do. I'm sending Darren across the street to stay with Aunt Pat. He and Jimmy can play together while we fix this."

My mother and Coreen went upstairs with me to pack some clothes and toys, enough to keep me busy until the morning. I gathered up what I needed and the three of us quickly went downstairs without even glancing into Coreen's room where I had seen the mysterious figure before.

I walked over to Jimmy's house with my little suitcase in hand. Aunt Cookie unpacked my stuff in their sunroom where Jimmy and I began to set up our toys. I had brought along a bunch of action figures made by a company called Mego, which manufactured the Planet of the Apes line of figures and accessories.

They were all contained in a pretty sizeable box along with a fortress, a working catapult and eight plastic boulders. Jimmy and I would spend the next few hours finding creative ways to kill each others apes with various boulders and catapults.

Later that night, just before ten o'clock, we washed up, got into our pajamas and went downstairs to catch re-runs of the *"Outer Limits"* TV show which was one of our personal favorites.

Although we normally wouldn't have been allowed to stay up so late, we used the excitement and confusion over the events across the street to our advantage.

We watched an entertaining episode entitled *"The Invisible Enemy"* starring the same actor who played Batman on the TV show. Before the show had even ended we were asleep with thoughts of outer space filling our dreams.

Back at our house across the street, the events were just beginning. My mom had decided to call in her friend Mrs. Thompson, whose family also lived just down the street.

The Thompson's had been family friends of ours for many years, and I frequently hung out with their two boys; George, who was the same age as Coreen, and Rich who was the same age as me.

My mother explained our situation to Mrs. Thompson who then began to tell her own story about an incident that had occurred while visiting our house the week before.

"While you and I were in the kitchen talking, George and Rich were sitting on the couch in the family room watching TV when suddenly George felt something strike him in the back as if he had been punched through the sofa cushions.

Rich said that George's whole body was nearly knocked off the couch from the force of the blow. Startled, they both tried to get off the couch but couldn't. They said they felt like they were being held in place by their ankles. They both sat back quickly and waited a few moments, then they were able to stand and move again.

"Oh my goodness!" my mother replied, "That's incredible!"

"Yes, but that's not all." Replied Mrs. Thompson. "Later

that afternoon when we returned home, George and Rich were in the kitchen talking about what had happened at your house earlier that day when suddenly all of the lights turned on and the electrical appliances began running all by themselves. Next, the cabinet doors began to open and close and, if that wasn't enough, the silverware drawer popped open and silverware started flying across the room!"

My mother gasped in surprise. She had not yet experienced such supernatural violence.

Mrs. Thompson continued, "And you know what made it even weirder? The appliances weren't even plugged in and several of the light bulbs that were shinning brightly had actually burned out weeks ago and hadn't been replaced!"

My mother's reply was cut short when the phone suddenly went dead. She hung it up, then picked it up again after a few seconds to check for a dial tone. Everything seemed to be working correctly and she was about to call Mrs. Thompson back when Aunt Cookie showed up.

The two women were exchanging greetings when Mrs. Thompson knocked on the door – she had come right over after the phone call ended so abruptly, fearing that something bad might have happened. "Is everyone all right?" she asked.

"Yes, we're all fine" my mother replied, "Let's pour ourselves a drink and get started – and after the day I've had, I may pour several." she laughed.

CHAPTER FIVE

OUIJA BOARD

My mother laid the Ouija board on top of the dining room table and the four women in attendance sat down to begin the séance. Mom placed her hands on the planchette, or pointer, which in this case was in the shape of a golden heart. Mrs. Thompson and Cookie followed suit with each of them holding an edge of the heart lightly with just the tips of their fingers. Coreen was armed with a pencil and pad of paper in the event contact with an actual spirit was made.

Immediately strange things began to happen. All the lights in the house started to switch themselves on and off at random. This included the lights in the barn, the garage, the pool house behind the garage and the exterior flood lights which surrounded the property. The unexpected light show continued for several minutes.

Even with all the action occurring around them, the four women didn't lose their concentration.

My mother, obviously sensing a spiritual presence, began to speak.

"Who are you?" she asked in a clear and confident tone.

The golden heart quickly slid over a series of letters spelling out the word, "E N O C H."

"Where are you from?" My mother asked.

There was no answer, nor was there any movement.

My mother continued, "Why are you in our home?"

Again the heart picked out letters. This time more rapidly than before. So quickly in fact that Coreen could barely write the letters down fast enough. She managed to spell out, "T H I S I S M Y H O U S E."

"What do you want?" mom asked next.

"A L L   M U S T   L E A V E." was the reply.

My mother answered quickly, "But we don't want to leave, can we come to some sort of agreement?"

The response – "D E A L ?"

My mom began to speak in Latin gleaned from her many years of Catholic school upbringing. Enoch replied in the same language. Since my mother was the only one at the table who spoke Latin, the deal would stay a secret between her and Enoch.

With the last letter having been written, there seemed to be no further response forthcoming from the board.

Again the lights began to flicker on and off followed by all of them coming on at once and burning unusually bright, almost as if it were daylight.

With barely a flinch, everyone at the table tried to remain focused and calm. My mom signed off and moved the gold heart over the Good Bye icon as the lights suddenly returned to normal. For the moment, all was calm.

As the women began chatting amongst themselves and prepared to leave, my mother turned to Coreen and said, in a very serious tone, "If you ever play with this thing, make sure that you sign off. We don't want to run the risk of making this thing any stronger than it already is."

Mom saw everyone out the door and then headed up to bed. It had been a trying day to say the least and she had difficulty falling asleep, tossing and turning until finally falling into a restless slumber. Then, around three o'clock in the morning she awoke coughing and hacking – the room seemed to be full of smoke!

She quickly sat upright in bed, her chest tightening as she coughed and struggled to breathe. It was hot – intensely hot, as if the door to the huge furnace had been flung wide open. Panicking, she dropped to the floor and began to crawl towards the door, but her movements were slow and lethargic as if in a dream. She struggled to move, but her body did not want to obey. Still, she continued to move forward, with an intense will to survive, weakly clawing ahead inch by inch, until she was stopped by an explosive, unnaturally powerful blast of heat.

Within seconds, she was incinerated, but for one awful moment in time – as her eyes melted and her flesh peeled away in burning strips – she was still alive, still conscious, still able to feel pain. In her final moment of life, she tried to scream with whatever breath she had left in her lungs.

"AAAAAHHHHHHHHH!!!!!!!!!!!"

Coreen, awakened instantly out of her deep slumber, immediately bolted out of her bed and ran down the hall towards the direction of the horrifying scream which seemed to have come from mom's room. She slammed open the door to see our mother lying dazed on the floor, soaked in sweat.

"What happened?" Coreen asked, helping her to her feet. "Are you all right?"

"Y... Yes, I'm fine, it was just... just a bad dream."

For the first time, Coreen noticed how warm it was in the room, hot actually, with a faint smoky odor, like a wood fire.

From that night on, our mother would often have similar nightmares. Although she would never speak about them openly, some mornings we could tell that she was a little more upset than usual and if questioned, she would begrudgingly admit to having another one of those awful dreams.

The next morning I returned home from Cousin Jimmy's and all seemed normal. Mom and Coreen were awake and eating breakfast at the dining room table. Both seemed to be in a good mood, so I asked "Anything happen last night?"

As my mother started to speak, I noticed how tired and worn she looked. "I don't think we'll be having any more problems for a while. Some spirits just get a little possessive and I think that this one needed a good talking to." she said.

Later that afternoon when Coreen and I were alone, I asked, "So what really happened last night?"

"It was so cool," Coreen answered, "I wish you were there. We found out that his name was Enoch or something and he said "This is my house", and mom said "No it's not!" and then the lights started going on and off and stuff. Then mom started talking to it in another language but I can't really remember anything she said, it's all kind of hazy."

Coreen and I would never end up getting a full explanation regarding what my mom said to the spirit, but whatever she said or did, it seemed to work. For the next several years, most of the major supernatural events came to an end. Although the spirit was never fully cast out, it did seem to honor the deal – an unholy pact between the living and the dead.

Of course, this didn't mean an end to *all* the strange behavior. Coreen and I had become quite accustomed to events such as the lights turning on and off and the dimmer switch on the chandelier spinning by itself, turning the room from darkness to blinding light, then back to darkness again.

We soon learned to take events like these in stride, even joking about them sometimes, saying things like "Boy he's really frisky tonight." or "Must not have gotten his exercise today!"

But whether we tried to ignore it or just laugh it off, we

still knew that something was very wrong with this house. There was definitely an evil presence that was continually trying to make itself known. For what reason though, was never really understood until a much later date.

Although I didn't realize it at the time, my father was also experiencing some unwanted psychological effects courtesy of the house, but kept it to himself. He dealt with his dilemma the same way the previous resident had – with alcohol.

Regardless of the cause, we couldn't help but notice that the drinking was slowly consuming him and would soon culminate in a near tragedy that would tear our family apart.

It began sometime after midnight one frigid February evening. My father arrived home very depressed and slightly intoxicated. He entered the den and settled into his worn leather chair which was situated behind his handmade rock maple desk. He opened our large family bible to page six. Under the heading "Deaths", there were a number of horizontal lines where one could write the names of family members and close friends who had died. Since it was a fairly new bible, there were no entries on the page as of yet.

My father reached for his good writing pen, a handmade walnut fountain pen with gold engraved trim. Steady and deliberately he began to write. In column one, "Name of the Deceased", he wrote his own name – Barry Fitzgerald.

In column two, "Died On:", he wrote the current date – February 27th, 1978. Then on the bottom half of the page, he quickly but carefully wrote his last will and testament which, quite simply, left the house and all his worldly possessions to his wife and children.

With his final task now complete, he put down his pen and opened the bottom right desk drawer from which he retrieved a bottle and a large glass which he placed directly in front of him. Continuing his slow, deliberate movements, he opened a small ice bucket which he had brought with him from the kitchen and carefully put two cubes in the glass. He then poured himself three fingers of his favorite 12 year old, single malt Scotch Whiskey.

For the first time that night, the corners of his mouth began to form a smile as he leaned back in his creaking leather chair and swirled his drink, listening contentedly as the ice clinked softly against the sides of the glass. He savored every sip as he slowly emptied the glass, reflecting back on the good times he had experienced in his life… and also the bad.

Finally he put down the glass and again, reached into the bottom drawer where this time, he pulled out a .45 caliber semi-automatic pistol and checked the action. Straightening up in his chair, he slowly placed the gun to his temple.

My father's hand shook as he began to squeeze the trigger. He knew that it only took six pounds of pressure to release the hammer and fire the gun, but just as his finger's pull reached about five pounds, he jerked the gun away, causing it to fire straight through the ceiling.

With the hot, smoking gun still clutched in his hand, he collapsed onto the desk and began to weep.

The noise from the shot was so loud that it woke up my aunt and uncle across the street. Uncle Egon knew the sound of a gunshot when he heard it and quickly called the police who arrived within minutes with lights blazing.

At that point my mother was screaming and cursing at my father accusing him of drinking too much and feeling sorry for himself, and so on, and so on until the policeman interrupted.

"Uh, ma'am, where exactly did the bullet go?"

Everyone's head turned upward to look at the ceiling.

"That's where Darren's room is!" My mother exclaimed, suddenly realizing the new found gravity of the situation.

Everyone quickly ran upstairs to see if I was alright. Thankfully I was; in fact, I was still sleeping. I had been lying on my side at the time as the bullet shattered through the floorboards, the box spring, and the mattress, just missing my lower spine. The hole went right through the center of the bed. Had I had been lying on my back at the time, I probably would have been killed or even worse, paralyzed for life.

Thankfully, there were no arrests made that night, but the police demanded that my father turn over all of his weapons. There were a total of six guns removed from our house that night. Then, in one final act of independence, my mother decided to remove herself from the marriage as well that very same evening.

CHAPTER SIX

WRITING ON THE WALL

For the next several months my sister and I were forced to stay with our grandparents while our mother and father worked out the details of their divorce. Even though we were living over five miles away, we would still visit our house on Hurley Pond Road on a regular basis.

One of the biggest attractions for us was our beautiful swimming pool. We had it installed the previous year but by the end of summer 1979, the pool had turned to a light shade of green. At first we thought it was either algae or some kind of chemical imbalance, but whatever we tried, we were unsuccessful in clearing it up. We replaced the filter, added extra chlorine and algaecides, adjusted the pH, but nothing seemed to work and in less than a weeks time, the water had turned to a dark emerald shade of green, almost approaching black towards the bottom. We called in several pool companies to take a look but their luck was no better than ours. They did however all agree on one thing – none of them had ever seen anything like it before.

Immediately following Labor Day weekend, my father stopped by with his box of tools to set about closing the pool for the season. My sister and I helped him out as best we could but mostly we just seemed to be in his way. After placing the weights on the perimeter of the pool cover and tying down the last strap to hold it in place for the winter my father stopped, pointed at the bright shiny blue pool cover and said jokingly, "Look kids, no more green pool!"

We all had a good laugh as we walked our dad back to his car. It had been a fun-filled afternoon but as he pulled away and said goodbye, I felt a great uneasiness – something wasn't quite right. I chose to shrug it off and headed back into the house.

I told my mom that we had finished closing the pool for the season with dad's help. She thanked me and asked if I could help her out by going up to the attic to bring down the Halloween decorations. Although Halloween was still over a month away, it had always been one of our favorite holidays so we liked to start as early as possible.

As I made my way upstairs, I stopped in to visit Coreen to ask if she might be able to lend a hand. She agreed and we headed off down the hall. As we rounded the corner, we noticed that the stairs had already been pulled down from the ceiling by what we assumed was our mother earlier in the day but I didn't like the look of it just the same.

"Okay Darren, you climb up there and I'll wait down here so I can catch the boxes as you hand them to me." Coreen said.

I of course replied with "I've got a better idea. Why don't *you* go up there and *I'll* wait down here to catch the boxes that you hand me?"

"Cause I'm older, that's why." she replied, visibly annoyed. "End of discussion."

There was more going on here than just idle sibling rivalry at this point. We both were a little uncomfortable with going into that attic alone – no real reason I suppose, just a general feeling of unease.

After quickly losing my verbal joust with my sister, I reluctantly trudged up the rickety staircase and pulled a string suspended from the ceiling to turn on the measly 40 watt overhead light bulb. There in the far left corner was the stack of Halloween boxes. Just my luck that it was the *farthest* corner of the attic. Why couldn't our mother just stack the stuff right next to the hatch opening where the Christmas stuff was placed?

I angrily picked my way over to where the Halloween

boxes were located, stepping over all manner of stuff that should have been sold in the last yard sale or more likely, simply tossed in the garbage. Then out of nowhere, I suddenly got the sensation of a chill in the air – almost as if the air-conditioner had been turned on. Trying to ignore the unusual sensation, I hastily lined up the boxes in a single row and pushed them all at once towards the open stairway hatch.

I quickly handed the boxes through the opening to Coreen, one at a time, but as I handed her the final box, I began to feel an intense coldness on the back of my neck, almost as if an icy hand were touching me. I quickly tossed the last box to Coreen and literally jumped down the stairs, missing her by inches.

Coreen looked at me and said, "What the heck's wrong with you?"

I mumbled something about my imagination getting the best of me and quickly grabbed a couple of boxes and headed downstairs; not even bothering to look back towards the attic or closing the stairs.

Coreen brought the rest of the boxes down to the living room, where we unpacked the decorations and laid them out on the floor. Halloween was just as important to us as Christmas in our family. Not only was it the season for trick-or-treating, but it was my father's birthday as well.

As Halloween approached, our home was slowly transformed into a house of horrors. Thankfully just fake ones this time around, with a number of hanging plastic ghosts, skeletons, bats, hidden loudspeakers emitting creepy sound effects, and the obligatory assortment of cobwebs, spiders and tombstones. As usual, our display was a hit with the local trick-or-treating crowd who would come from miles around to see our display.

But before every Halloween there was another minor holiday which added to the excitement of the season. October 30th, the night before Halloween is commonly known as mischief night in this part of the country. Its when groups of kids get together and set about toilet papering people's yards, egging cars, writing on windows with soap, smashing pumpkins and getting into a whole host of troubles, all in the name of harmless fun.

But this night there would be no mischief making. Instead I met my friend Jack at his house around six o'clock on Saturday evening. He excitedly told me that we were both in for a treat that night. "You know what they're showing down at the local theater as the double feature tonight? *Godzilla vs the Smog Monster* and *Night of the Living Dead*!" he eagerly exclaimed.

It sounded like the makings of a fun night to me so we began our trek to the town of Belmar, following the muddy banks of the Shark River and on through to McLeary Park. As we walked, the sky began to turn gray and the wind picked up as if a storm were approaching. The temperature seemed to have fallen about ten degrees in as many minutes.

Upon reaching the park, we scampered up the stone retaining wall which separated the park from the river and continued on our journey. As we walked through the tree lined path, we noticed some small, green pieces of paper blowing in the wind towards us. As they got closer I realized what they actually were. It was a bunch of single dollar bills – twenty to be exact. Ten for each of us!

We gathered up whatever we could find and ran happily across the park to the marina where we slowed back down to a walk. Jack and I continued to talk about our luck and what a great night it was going to be.

Before we arrived at the theater, we took a few minute detour to stop in to see Jack's parents who were working at the small dry cleaner which they owned and operated. Jack, making no mention of the twenty dollars we just came upon, hit his parents up for yet another twenty so that we could go to the movies. His parents, not aware of the slightly under-handed ruse, gladly obliged.

With money in hand, we quickly said our good-byes and made our way over to Shatsow's five-and-dime store. We took a look at the various discounted Halloween items but finding nothing of interest there, headed on over to the action figure aisle. Star Wars was still very much in the mind of the average eleven year old back then as we were all looking forward to seeing *The Empire Strikes Back* the following spring. I ended up spending my not so hard earned money on an R2D2 and Darth Vader figurine while Jack picked up the Obi-Wan Kenobi and C3PO toys.

By now the movie was only minutes away from starting so we quickly paid the cashier and hurried over to the theater.

We made it in the nick of time and as we waited in line, I happened to notice the posters for *Night of Living Dead* adorning the walls. That was the afternoon I became a die-hard horror fan. *Godzilla vs. the Smog Monster* was cool, in a comical sort of way, but it was the *Night of the Living Dead* that I enjoyed the most. It was the first movie to really scare the hell out of me. Jack and I spent most of our walk home that night doing our best zombie imitations and discussing how we should be planning our defenses for the eventual day when the dead would rise up and take over the earth.

After Halloween ended, my family and I reluctantly took down our decorations and packed them away without incident.

Things seemed to stay calm up until late November – three days before Thanksgiving to be exact. Our mother was getting ready to spend the holiday with her new boyfriend Cliff Underwood. Cliff was a real man's man, a rugged ex-ranger from Tennessee who reminded us of John Wayne, right down to his southern drawl.

Cliff was treating my mother to an overnight Thanksgiving weekend in upstate New York, leaving Coreen and my cousin Tammy in charge of the house until they returned.

As mom loaded her luggage into Cliff's car, our cousins Tammy and Lisa arrived.

My grandmother was already on her way to pick me up so I could spend the weekend with her and Pop-Pop. While waiting for her to arrive, Lisa and I decided to go downstairs to the basement to play with the train set that my father had built several years ago. It was a large and extremely detailed 'N' gauge model railroad set with what seemed like miles of track winding through majestic mountains made of plaster and miniature evergreen forests.

Lisa and I entered the oversized "train room" where I quickly sat down at the controls. Soon the Union Express was pulling out of the station and quickly picked up speed as it rounded a bend before disappearing into a tunnel.

Lisa wanted to see how fast it could go, so I pushed the lever forward to full speed. We had a great time joking and laughing as we watched it race around the track until suddenly Lisa's head snapped up and said, "Did you hear that?"

"What?" I replied as I pulled back on the lever, bringing the train to a full stop.

In the silence that followed, I heard the sound too – a faint hissing sound, like air escaping from a bicycle tire.

Deciding to investigate, we headed out the door towards

the source of the noise, stopping suddenly as we rounded the corner. There on the wall, no more than ten feet in front of us was a message spray painted in bright red letters:

COREEN, LISA, TAMMY, JIMMY. I WILL KILL YOU!!!

From the back of the room, a spray paint can slowly rolled toward us, the paint still wet on the nozzle. I stopped it with my foot, as it came to rest.

"Look Darren, on the other wall..."

There on the adjacent wall, in gold paint was my name in large capital letters. Next to it, on the blackboard which was hanging from the wall was a single word HELLO written in white chalk.

We immediately ran upstairs to tell my mother and her and Cliff quickly came down to assess the situation.

After a moment my mother said, "Your father must have done this – probably drinking again – he's the only one who writes like that."

Lisa and I knew better but said nothing. Instead we gathered up some turpentine and rags and began to clean off the graffiti while Cliff set about searching the house and grounds for anything out of the ordinary.

After we had finished cleaning the graffiti off the wall, my mother put down her paint soaked rags and went upstairs to call my father's office. Fully expecting him not to be there she was surprised when he picked up on the first ring. There was no way he could have been here to paint the walls and gotten back to his office that quickly my mother thought. She engaged him in some meaningless small talk and then quickly said goodbye.

A few minutes later, Cliff returned. He had searched the house from top to bottom for any sign of intruders, but found nothing.

After determining that there was nothing left they could do and all seemed safe, Cliff and my mom got into his new pickup and restarted their trip to New York.

I sat waiting on the porch for my grandmother to arrive to bring me back to her house in Bradley Beach. My mind had begun to drift when I was abruptly shaken out of my day-dreaming state by a car horn. My grandmother had arrived.

On the drive over I told her everything about what had happened. One of the great things about my grandmother was that I could tell her pretty much anything and she would just listen carefully and offer to help; never laughing or treating me like a child.

She was a strong willed person who believed in the supernatural but had an even greater faith in God. When we arrived at her house, she said, "Let's pray that Coreen is not in any sort of trouble…" but the ringing of the telephone cut her off in mid sentence. It was Coreen again and she sounded very upset. "It's all over the walls again!" she practically screamed.

"What's all over the walls?" my grandmother asked.

"The writing… in the basement, it's everywhere, it says, COREEN, LISA, TAMMY, JIMMY, PAT… I WILL KILL YOU!" Coreen replied, nearly in tears, "And in other places it says 'DARREN' and a bunch of other names I never heard of!"

"Alright Coreen, I'm coming back over to get you but for now, just get out of that house. You can wait out front for me." But before grandma could hang up, we heard a deep, demonic voice emanating from the phone saying simply "THE CHILDREN BELONG TO ME NOW!" then the line went dead.

Needless to say, we were terrified for Coreen's safety, so we quickly woke up my grandfather who drove us all back to the house As he drove we tried to bring him up to speed on the phone call and some of the other incidents that had occurred over the years as we raced back over to Hurley Pond Road.

We arrived, barely ten minutes later, to see Coreen and Tammy running from the porch towards our car which they quickly jumped into. We all returned safely to my grandmother's house where we would spend the night without further incident.

The next morning, Coreen and Tammy returned to Hurley Pond Road, but this time, they stayed at Tammy's house across the street. Still unsettled by the recent events, but curious just the same, they decided to try a session with the Ouija board, but there was one catch – it was still in our house across the street. After much deliberation they mustered enough courage to go back and quickly retrieve the board, practically running in and out like olympic sprinters.

Returning back to my cousin's house, Coreen, Tammy, and now Lisa set up the board on the dining room table. Tammy and Lisa held the string with the caret, while Coreen began the séance, asking if there were any spirits present. There was no reply, so she began asking random questions some of which were answered with brief yes or no answers, but most were not.

Then after about fifteen minutes the caret became very busy, spelling out letters as quickly as Coreen could write them down:

YOURE DEAD

YOURE ALL DEAD

The three girls looked at each other nervously, wondering what they should do next when they heard something scratching at the front door. They quickly packed up the Ouija board and threw it on top of the refrigerator.

A few seconds later Aunt Pat walked in, "What are you

girls up to?" she asked. "Why is everyone giving me a guilty look?"

"Oh, we were just playing a board game" Tammy replied, giggling, and the three girls hurried off upstairs to Tammy's room.

"That was really weird," said Tammy, "I thought Ouija boards were supposed to give vague, evasive answers – this one seemed to be pretty blunt!"

"I know!" Coreen replied, "I'm going to ask mom when she gets back, maybe she can help – she sure straightened things out last time she used the board!"

As night fell, the girls were making the most out of their sleep-over, laughing, gossiping and so on until well after midnight before finally deciding to settle down and start getting ready for bed.

As the lights went out the girls were still talking quietly amongst themselves when they suddenly heard footsteps walking back and forth on the creaking floorboards of the attic. The girls lied in their beds, both quiet and frightened as the steps continued until after two o'clock in the morning. Then all was silent.

The next day as Cliff and my mother returned from their trip they stopped off at grandma's house to pick me up. On the way back to Hurley Pond Road, I told my mom about the latest incident the day before involving Coreen and Tammy and the writing on the walls.

As soon as we pulled into the driveway, Coreen came running over from across the street, looking like she didn't sleep much the night before.

We all went inside and I got my first view of the latest writing – it was unbelievable. On nearly every wall was a message or someone's name written in red paint – only my name was in gold and I was not threatened with death as all the others were.

My mother looked around with a blank expression – I

couldn't tell if she was frightened, angry, or both. Cliff didn't know what to think, but being a man of action, he quickly gathered up some paint scrapers, turpentine, buckets and rags and ordered everyone to start cleaning.

We spent the next week scraping, and wiping paint from the walls, although some had to be entirely re-painted.

The whole thing put a damper on our moods as we entered into the Christmas season. For Coreen and I, this would be our first Christmas without our father living at home.

As the holiday approached, we set up the tree and decorations as if nothing were wrong, and for the most part, nothing was.

About a week before Christmas, my uncle Jimmy stopped over with gifts for the family. I always looked forward to uncle Jimmy's gifts. He seemed to understand that kids didn't want clothes or shoes or anything practical – we wanted toys!

What he brought that day was a two-foot long model of the Goodyear blimp, made by Revell. According to the picture on the box, the blimp was supposed to light up and electronic messages would scroll around the sides, just like the real thing.

Uncle Jimmy spent several minutes with Coreen and I making small talk, then disappeared into the kitchen to spend some time with my mom. While they were talking, I went right to work on my new model, which uncle Jimmy didn't even bother to wrap, knowing that I would probably open it immediately and not wait until Christmas.

By now it was getting pretty late; close to seven o'clock in fact and Uncle Jimmy was preparing to leave. He still had to make two more stops before he was able to go home and call it a day.

I went back to my zeppelin model, which I had set up on a bunch of old newspapers on the dinning room table. Most of the parts were already trimmed and painted so final assembly was about to begin. As I sat at the table, watching the light from the fireplace flicker on the blimp's polished surface, I felt quite happy and content, and for a moment, I was able to forget all of the strange and disturbing things that had been happening recently in our house.

After gazing thoughtfully into the fireplace for a few more minutes, I began to assemble the blimp. I connected the two halves of the zeppelin, gluing the edges and holding the parts together with rubber bands. As I snapped the last rubber band into place, I heard the den door open slowly with a slightly creepy creaking sound, straight out of your typical haunted house movie. I looked over at the door but saw nothing at first. Then I noticed something moving along the floor which caught my eye. It was my mother's bowling trophy sliding out of the den and along the floor seemingly under its own power. I blinked my eyes a few times to make sure I wasn't seeing things, then called out to my mother.

"Look at this!" I said as she entered the dining room. I pointed to the den door where her trophy was now accompanied by others, each sliding into the room in a single file through the door. First were my mom's bowling trophies, four in all, followed by Coreen's six soccer trophies, each filing out of the den in a slow procession.

"Maybe he's jealous of our athletic ability." my mom joked, "The poor thing has no trophies of its own!"

But as we all started to laugh, the trophies began to smash into each other violently, breaking the arms and legs off the gold plastic figurines that were mounted on top. While this was happening, the chandelier over the dining room table suddenly began to brighten from a soft glow to blinding brilliance then went out completely – in fact, the power seemed to be out for the entire house, leaving only the soft glow of the fireplace as our only source of light.

We heard Coreen call out from her bedroom upstairs as she began making her way down to see what was happening.

As she entered the dining room, the power returned and the lights came back on.

We all looked at each other nervously, wondering if the spirit was done for the night, or if it still had more in store for us.

Our answer came in the form of a tremendous splashing sound coming from the den. I rushed to the doorway and there in our 50 gallon fish tank, was a large wooden bust of Thomas Jefferson that formerly resided on top of our father's desk. I plucked the bust from the water and dried it off as best I could with my shirt, and replaced it to its rightful place on his desk.

Coreen and my mom were now in the room with me, looking around for any other items that were out of place, when the door to the dinning room slammed shut violently. Immediately the books, several hundred of them in fact, started to fly off the shelves and rain down onto the floor. As the last book hit the cork flooring, the door to the dining room slowly reopened and a loud banging noise ensued. The banging seemed to come from the house itself, as if someone was pounding on the very walls and floors. The intense pounding grew louder and louder until we could no longer hear each other speak.

After about five more minutes of this constant commotion, there was finally silence. Mom, Coreen and I just looked at each other in a kind of weary astonishment. No matter how many times we experienced these types of events, we could never really get used to them. Each incident challenged everything we were taught to believe in and left us gasping in astonishment and fear.

It took us several hours to clean up the mess, but finally the den was back in order, looking none the worse. We all agreed to sleep downstairs in the dinning room that night, next to the fireplace.

"No one is to be alone at any time." my mother warned

us, "If you need something from the kitchen, we'll all go together, is that understood?"

Thankfully the night passed uneventfully. It was even kind of fun, in some respects; sort of like an indoor camping trip. For the next several days, nothing unusual happened; although as we would later find out, this was only the calm before the storm.

CHAPTER SEVEN

HOME FOR THE HOLIDAYS

It was now Christmas night 1979, but apparently the second holiest day on the Christian calendar did not seem to impress our guest, the one who called himself "Enoch." This particular holiday would go down as one of the most unforgettable days of my entire life – but not for any of the usual pleasant Christmas memories.

That morning found my mom, Coreen and myself in front of our Christmas tree exchanging gifts as a light snow began to fall outside. Even in this tranquil setting on Christmas morning at home with our family, we still found ourselves feeling anxious and walking on eggshells as we waited for the next shoe to drop. Living at this house, you always had to keep your guard up.

As the hours passed, Coreen and my mother busied themselves by tidying up the house, while I continued to play with some of the cool toys that I had received that very morning. The Micronauts, battery powered figurines alone were able to keep me busy for hours on end.

For a few moments, we were able to catch the holiday spirit, as friends and relatives begin arriving, bringing gifts, hugging and laughing, and getting ready for the big Christmas dinner.

After a few minutes of small talk with the grown-ups I retreated to the den where I had left my zeppelin model. With a little over an hour still left before dinner, I decided to sit down at the desk to add some finishing touches.

Soon, mom was calling everyone over to the table, which was covered with serving plates and festive centerpieces. During the past hour, several more guests had shown up bringing the total to twelve hungry people, all eager to start the feast.

The food had already been laid out on the table. Turkey, stuffing, yams, potatoes, rolls, cranberry sauce; just about all the traditional items were present – except for my dad.

My father always seemed to be able to make these holiday get-togethers a little more festive and his absence saddened me. But soon my thoughts were focused on the beautiful golden brown bird in front of me.

Before anyone could eat though, we would need to say grace. My uncle Jimmy stood at the head of the table and began to give the traditional Christmas blessing when suddenly the chandelier began to brighten to a brilliant, blinding glow.

Everyone stopped what they were doing and looked around the room uncomfortably. Most of the guests had heard about the strange events in the house but few had ever seen it for themselves.

Mom tried to distract everyone by beginning to pass the food – it didn't work.

The chandelier began to spin slowly in a counter-clockwise direction for about a minute then stopped.

As I looked around the table, everyone's eyes were wide with astonishment. My grandfather was still staring at the light, his jaw hanging open in disbelief.

Cliff's daughter Patty was the first to speak, "That was a little freaky!" she said with awe in her voice.

I replied, "Wait a few minutes. It's just getting started."

And sure enough, at that instant the chandelier began spinning so quickly that it wound up its cord and slammed into the ceiling, shattering most of the bulbs and contaminating the meal with splinters of glass.

Then, the swinging door to the kitchen began to swing back and forth on its own, speeding up until the door was just a blur. That was the last thing we were able to see clearly as all the lights in the house suddenly went out.

At first, no one moved, but Patty began to scream almost hysterically. I could see from the glow of the fireplace that she was in tears. Her brother Allen, sitting next to her, exclaimed, "Holy crap!" as he stood up and pointed to something moving along the floor, coming from the den. It was my zeppelin model; even though it had no wheels or power source, it was somehow sliding across the floor.

Midway into the room, it stopped and a message began scrolling across its LED side panel: "YOU ARE ALL DEAD!"

After pausing there for a few seconds, flashing its sadistic message, the model continued on through the room sliding along until it bumped into the presents underneath the Christmas tree.

At that moment the lights came back on, revealing the unfortunate aftermath of the formerly festive party.

Patty was still sobbing, and her brothers Mike and Allen were looking rather pale and shaken. Despite the fact that these two were a couple of big, rugged guys, who didn't believe in ghosts or the supernatural, they looked as if they had been reduced to a couple of scared little children. In an instant, they were quickly up from their chairs and out the front door, followed by their father Cliff.

Next, Aunt Helen and cousins Tammy and Lisa, also sobbing, said their hurried good-byes and left, practically begging us to come stay at their house.

My mother told Coreen and I to go with them, but we both declined. There was no way that I was going to leave my mom alone to deal with that thing, and Coreen fortunately, felt the same way.

As our grandparents prepared to leave, my grandmother told us that she would be back in the morning with some ideas, and some help.

As their car pulled out of the driveway, mom ordered us to our "beds" in front of the Christmas tree where we all stayed close, listening for anything unusual.

We all laid awake until the Westminster chimed twelve o'clock midnight. As soon as the chimes stopped, we heard a loud clicking noise coming from upstairs, followed by a hissing sound, and then four more clicks. I immediately recognized the sound; it was Coreen's 8-Track player.

Sure enough, the next thing we heard was music off of Alice Cooper's *"From the Inside"* album blaring forth from Coreen's stereo.

As soon as the music started, the chandelier began flickering on and off like a strobe light, keeping time to the rocking sounds of Alice Cooper.

The song played through, ending with a chorus of voices singing, "We're all crazy... We're all crazy... We're all crazy..." fading out to the end. We heard a few more clicks and the same song started to play again, and again...

Oddly enough, I found the music and flashing lights kind of entertaining – it was one of my all-time favorite songs. The music/light show continued on until about one in the morning, then all was silent, although I don't think anyone actually succeeded in falling asleep that night.

The next morning, my Aunt Helen and Lisa came over and wound up spending the entire day, which fortunately, proved to be uneventful. The women occupied themselves by cooking and gossiping while I tried to enjoy my presents under the tree, but there was an unmistakable cloud of fear hanging over all of us.

Playing with the toys seemed to help take my mind off of the events of the previous evening. Coreen and mom were always close by, watching and listening for anything unusual. My mind drifted into a world of play and for a few moments everything was back to normal.

Little did we realize that the next day it would start the earliest and become the most violent we had ever seen. The day began normally enough before it started with one door slamming – then another – and another.

It started in the basement and worked its way upstairs, slamming every door in the house; even the closets and cabinets.

Although we would soon get used to minor occurrences such as these, we were all gripped by fear at the moment as the deafening racket seemed to engulf the entire house. Each event felt like it would go on for hours, but in reality, only a few minutes would pass before the racket would end abruptly, replaced by an eerie silence.

Around noon mom's boyfriend Cliff stopped in, followed soon after by grandma Pickell, and finally Aunt Helen.

They all gathered in the family room, talking, laughing and hugging and once again tried to get into the Christmas spirit. I really didn't expect any more weird events with all the people standing around, but I soon found out that it was going to be just the opposite – it seemed to enjoy an audience – the more the merrier I guess.

But at the particular moment, things were calm as Coreen and I stood by ourselves in the living room, trying to forget about the recent strangeness as we casually sampled some of the desserts and pies that were laid out on the counter.

I was considering saying something about how quiet it was being this afternoon when I was interrupted by a long, creaking sound of a door being opened – the door from the dining room to the den.

As the creaking suddenly stopped, Coreen looked over at me and said, "Oh shit, here we go again."

"So much for this holiday season." I muttered, nearly jumping at the sound of the den door suddenly slamming shut.

This was followed immediately by a loud banging, as if a sledgehammer was being pounded against the walls, floors and ceilings, all at the same time. The noise seemed to come from everywhere, ringing loudly throughout the entire house, never pausing, but slowly becoming more intense.

With our ears covered, Coreen and I began walking towards the dining room. We were quickly joined by my grandmother who we motioned to follow us. As soon as we got in front of the den door – ready for anything – the deafening noise stopped as suddenly as it began. Then the door swung open by itself.

Coreen immediately walked in, while the rest of us hesitate outside, "Darren, you've got to see this!" she said excitedly.

The first thing I noticed as I peered inside, were the empty bookshelves. Fully expecting the books to be strewn across the floor, I was surprised to see them stacked neatly and intricately, like a house of cards, but on a much larger scale.

As I took a step towards the door I felt my grandmother's arm on my shoulder, holding me back. She said "Coreen, get out of there, I don't like the look of this…"

But as Coreen walked back toward us, she stopped suddenly just a few feet from the door. She looked at me and all she could say was "Darren, help."

She seemed to be struggling to move and as I looked closer, I saw the imprint of an arm around her waist, apparently holding her in place. As she struggled against her invisible assailant, her feet began to rise off the floor until she was at least a foot in the air. As I started to enter the den, the door slammed shut violently in my face, nearly breaking my nose. That's when my mother and Cliff rushed in.

We quickly told mom what had just happened and the three of us began pulling at the door. No matter how hard we tried, we were unable to get it to budge. At this point Coreen had been trapped in the room for nearly five minutes, and we could only listen helplessly to her cries of desperation on the other side of the door.

Surprisingly, or maybe not so surprisingly, it was my mother who took charge of the situation and suddenly screamed with far more anger than fear, saying "You open that door right now or I will kill myself and fight you on your own level – that's my daughter you son of a bitch!"

Immediately the door flew open, nearly breaking off of its hinges. We rushed into the room to find Coreen lying on the floor unconscious. Mom slapped her face lightly until she came to, but she was still unable to tell us anything about her ordeal. She claimed that she remembered nothing after being grabbed from behind and lifted off of her feet.

"I felt these invisible arms grabbing me so tightly that I could barely breathe. It lifted me right off the ground like I was a rag doll!"

Soon after that, the banging began anew, soft at first, then louder and louder until, once again, it was nearly deafening – "BANG… BANG… BANG!" The sound echoed throughout the house, rattling the windows and shaking the floors.

We had had enough. We rushed from the house as a group and into our cars – the plan was to get to my grandmother's and stay there for at least the evening. Coreen and I gathered up some of our belongings while mom fed the dogs, hating to leave them there by themselves.

Cliff pulled out of the driveway first, followed by my grandmother. My mother, Coreen and I were situated in the last vehicle. As we followed, I looked back at the house in amazement from the relative safety of our car. The house lights were going on and off at random while the doors continued to open and slam shut. Even the heavy wooden doors of the barn were opening and closing rapidly, while the garage doors slid noisily up and down.

Then as the wind suddenly picked up, all the lights, from

the basement to the attic, went on and stayed on while all the doors opened and stayed open, allowing the terrified dogs to escape.

My mom said "Let them go, they won't go very far and we can get them back tomorrow." But then, one by one, the five horses also began to leave the barn and walk away.

Now we had a real problem; a couple of loose dogs roaming around the neighborhood was one thing but five large horses on the loose was quite another. We turned our cars around and pulled back into the driveway to deal with the situation.

Grandma and Cliff soon returned to see why we had come back. They joined up with my mother, sister and I as we all began leading the horses back to their stalls. We managed to get the animals back to where they belonged and then padlocked all their gates and doors.

We got back into our respective cars and began to leave once again. I saw that the activity in the barn had returned to normal, but the house was still seemingly engulfed in paranormal activity. The doors were opening and closing while the lights continued to flicker on and off.

The difference now was that some of the small stones that lined the front steps were flying through the air and pelting Cliff's truck along with the other vehicles in the driveway. The last thing I saw as we pulled out, was the doors of the house rhythmically opening and closing as if the whole house were breathing.

When we reached my grandmother's house, we looked at each other but could say nothing. I looked up at my mom and saw a woman who thought she had everything but now slowly realizing that it had all become worthless.

The next day, my mom tried to find a house to rent. She located a property a few miles away but we weren't able to move in until after the New Year which was still three days away.

So once again we begrudgingly returned to our house on Hurley Pond Road in order to pack up our belongings. With the help of our cousins we managed to box up just about all of our essentials by the end of the afternoon

Jimmy, Tammy, Lisa and Cliff packed up the entire kitchen, except for the silverware drawer, along with all the books in the den. Coreen and I were with grandma in my room while Helen was in Coreen's room – no one was to be left alone at any time.

The day passed without incident and soon we had everything packed and ready to go. Aunt Helen and my cousin located the dogs and took them to their house while we went back to stay at my grandmother's house for the night.

The next day we arrived early to begin moving the previously packed boxes back to our grandmother's house. As we walked into the kitchen, we saw that the contents of the refrigerator had been spilled across the floor along with a message written for us in ketchup: "COREEN, TAMMY, LISA, PAT, JIMMY – YOU ARE ALL DEAD".

Mom tried to shine a little humor on the situation by saying, "At least it'll be easier to clean up this time . . ." but she began to weep before completing the sentence. Coreen and I walked over to try to comfort her.

She looked at us and said, "You kids are the best damn thing that ever happened to me. Without you two I would probably just collapse."

Then the banging sound began again but quickly subsided. What followed next was a new sound which sounded like water running in the basement. We all ran downstairs at once to investigate; a move that was more than a little scary since I was worried that the thing might try to trap us all in the basement as it had trapped Coreen in the den only a few days before.

As we passed the train set and headed down the long corridor, we saw water pooling on the floor which was flowing towards us rather rapidly. It seemed to be coming from the wine cellar where we could hear what sounded like water hissing from a broken pipe. As we opened the wine cellar door, I noticed that one of the exposed pipes near the ceiling had a large crack in it. I could also see that the shutoff valve was just to the right of the crack. At this point, my mother, Coreen and grandma were watching through the doorway as there wasn't much room inside for more than one person at a time.

It would seem like a simple task to shut off the valve and stop the water, but it would prove otherwise. As I reached the end of the long rows of wine bottles, I was able to find an empty wooden wine crate, so covered with cobwebs that it appeared white. I placed the box under the pipe and carefully climbed up to reach the valve.

With water spraying me in the face and soaking me from head to toe, I finally managed to get the rusted old valve closed, which succeeded in stopping the flow of water. I turned to the doorway and told everyone, "See, nothing to it!" but as I stepped off of the crate, the door slammed shut and all the lights went out.

Before I knew it I was on the floor, struggling to get up. It was as if an incredibly strong force was trying to hold me down. I managed to get partially back on my feet before being slammed into the wine racks. The force knocked several bottles to the floor, shattering them on impact.

I swung my arms wildly, trying to hit whatever was attacking me, but only connected with air. Suddenly I was struck hard in the sternum which knocked the wind out of me. As I struggled to catch my breath, I was hit again, this time square in the face, splitting my upper lip. I felt the warmth of blood against my cold wet skin as I struggled for my life against the unseen assailant.

Suddenly the struggle ceased and all the lights slowly brightened, as if they were on a dimmer switch. As my eyes adjusted to the dim light I saw the outline of what appeared to be a large man with his back to me, facing the door. As I blinked my eyes the image vanished and the cellar door opened.

Coreen rushed in and grabbed me by the shoulders, "Oh my God, what did it do to you?" she asked as she saw the blood flowing from my lip.

She led me out of the cellar by my hand and as we crossed the threshold, the door slammed shut and we began to hear the sound of rushing water again. Still dazed, I looked at my mother and all I could think to say was, "You'd better call a plumber."

With all of us safely back in the kitchen my mom set about calling the local plumber A fellow named Joe answered the phone and told us that he'd be here in a couple of hours. In the meantime, we should try to locate the main shutoff valve and close it. Mom knew better than to try and explain the real situation, so we decided to let the water run until the plumber arrived.

In the meantime, we started loading some of the previously packed boxes into our car. We put the smaller boxes in grandma's car, while the larger ones went into the back of Cliff's pickup truck.

Just as we were finishing our first load, the plumber arrived. My mother escorted him down to the wine cellar and within an hour, the repairs were complete. When the plumber left, my cousin and grandmother also left to go back to her house and unload the first round of boxes.

By now it was going on mid afternoon. The three of us were busily stacking boxes on the slate porch while waiting for my cousin and grandmother to return. Following each box stacking ritual in the cold December air, we would run back into the dining room and stand by the fireplace in order to warm back up.

One time as we were waiting by the fire, making idle chatter, there was a sudden loud crash from upstairs. We rushed up the stairs and opened the door to Coreen's room where the noise seemed to have come from. We were greeted by the sight of Coreen's stereo on the floor as well as several of her stuffed animals.

As we were surveying the damage, the floral patterned wallpaper began to peel itself off of the walls. Each strip would curl down upon itself and fall to the floor, one after the other. As this was happening, the bed suddenly began to rise into the air to a height of about four feet. Then it began to rotate slowly like a rotisserie.

Terrified, we all ran back downstairs and out the front door, almost slamming into our cousin who had just arrived. As soon as we started to tell him what was going on upstairs in Coreen's room, we heard my grandmother scream. We rushed back into the kitchen and saw that the silverware drawer had been opened and all the knives and utensils were currently sticking out of the wall just behind her.

"The drawer opened by itself and everything flew out at me!" grandma cried. I looked at the wall in amazement – every single utensil was stuck in the wall, even the spoons!

Grandma, who was closest to the back door said "Let's get the heck out of here!" and quickly walked out with us following close behind. But as soon as she stepped outside, the back door slammed shut locking us in. As we stood there, trying unsuccessfully to get the door unlocked, the rest of the doors in the house all slammed shut at once and locked themselves. We raced around to each of the first floor rooms, trying every exterior door and window but nothing would budge.

Sometimes when you watch an old horror movie where the victims are trapped inside a house you ask yourself, why don't they just break a window to get out? Well I grabbed one of the solid oak dinning room chairs and threw it against the window with all my might, but it just bounced off as if it was protected by some kind of invisible barrier.

But with no other options readily available, Coreen and I decided to venture into the living room to try to smash out the big bay window which overlooked the side yard. As we walked through the doorway the heavy drapes that hung over the bay window suddenly closed themselves followed by a rush of cold air that seemed to be surrounding us.

By now, our mom had arrived in the living room just in time to see the furniture beginning to rise into the air, finally settling at just above eye level. Mom turned around and gasped at what was happening in the dining room at the same time.

The dining room table and chairs were also suspended in midair. In fact, as we looked around the house, every box or piece of furniture was levitating, quietly floating in space. Our mother, with a very determined look on her face, walked right up to the drapes and with her rage overpowering her fear, pulled them apart violently. My heart nearly stopped as I saw a face looking back at us from outside the window!

To my relief, it was only grandma who was trying to get our attention. "I'm going to get some help!" she yelled and then ran across the street to my cousin's house.

Mom, Coreen and I returned to the kitchen and waited by the outside door. After a few minutes grandma returned telling us that no one was home across the street. She tried the door handle again and much to our surprise it actually opened! Within seconds, we could hear all the doors in the house unlocking themselves and opening.

Grandma asked, "Are you guys alright? Let's get out of here!"

But Coreen answered, "No, this is our house and I'm not leaving until we finish moving our stuff."

So we, very quickly this time, managed to move the remaining boxes and most of the smaller furniture out of the house by the time darkness fell. As we loaded our dogs into the car, we heard the chimes of our Westminster grandfather clock strike eight times.

By now our cousins across the street had finally returned home. Lisa and Jimmy walked over and asked if they could come in to take one last look at our house since they knew that we would most likely be moving out for good.

My mother replied "Look kids, things have gotten way out of control over here and I just don't think it's safe right now." She continued, "I'm just afraid that someone might get hurt, or even killed!"

But Jimmy said that he needed to use the bathroom badly, so Mom and Coreen escorted him to the downstairs bathroom and stood guard outside the door. After a few moments, they heard the toilet flush which was immediately followed by a scream. The door flew open and Jimmy ran out, nearly knocking over my mother.

"There was a face looking at me from outside the window, just standing there staring at me!" Jimmy wailed.

We tried to look out the window, but were unable to see anything in the darkness so we all returned to the dining room.

As we stood by the table, the lights began to go out and the doors started slamming shut again, one at a time, starting downstairs and moving upwards until every door in the house was shut.

Next, the banging started, lasting only a few seconds this time around, after which all was silent. Shortly thereafter the doors began to reopen, once again starting downstairs and working their way upwards. However the lights still remained off.

Seizing our opportunity to escape, we all ran through the kitchen towards the back door but as soon as we got close, the door slammed shut and the deadbolt snapped into the locked position – it looked as if we are trapped once again!

Suddenly Lisa screamed and as we turned to look, we saw the figure of a very tall man approaching us slowly from the darkened family room. He got to within 15 feet of us when he suddenly dropped into a sprinter's stance as if he was about to charge us. The mysterious figure lurched forward towards us, and then simply disappeared, leaving an ice-cold blast of air in his wake.

At that moment, all the lights came back on and the deadbolt on the back door slid open. Everyone rushed outside as my mom and I stayed behind a moment longer to herd the dogs out although they needed little encouragement. I had always suspected that they could sense that something wasn't right with this house from the moment we moved in.

We all piled into the pickup truck and locked the doors. Mom was in the driver's seat with me in the middle and Lisa on the end. Coreen and our dogs were in the back.

Mom put the key into the ignition, but in this case, the engine wouldn't turn over. As we sat there motionless in the driveway, the house began its usual display of flashing lights and slamming doors, but this time the light show was accompanied by a powerful wind which rose and fell, rocking our pickup truck violently from side to side.

Suddenly our car door locks mysteriously popped up, unlocking all the doors. Mom and Lisa pushed them back down, but they would instantly pop up again. After several more attempts, they just gave up.

Next the windows began to open and close by themselves. These were not electric windows by the way, but somehow the handles were spinning on their own.

While mom, Lisa and I were absorbed with watching the out of control windows, Coreen was the first to notice the latest threat.

"Mom, what's happening to the driveway!" she screamed.

We all looked up to see the packed gravel driveway behaving more like the surface of the ocean. Four or five ripples of gravel were heading towards us from the end of the driveway, but as they drew nearer, the ripples merged into one large wave of rocks that crashed into the back of our pickup.

Coreen crouched over the dog and covered her head as the wave hit, showering her with hundreds of little pebbles.

At that same moment, all the windows in the truck shattered, covering us with millions of tiny diamond like pieces of safety glass. As we sat there looking at each other with dazed expressions on our faces, both of the car doors suddenly flew open. Lisa was ripped out of her seat by some unseen force and started to get dragged backwards towards the house. She must have been dragged nearly twenty feet before the unseen force abruptly stopped, letting her fall to the ground.

Coreen managed to get out of the back of the truck pretty much unscathed, as were my mother and I. We rushed over to where Lisa was laying. She was pretty shaken up but otherwise okay.

While we were tending to Lisa, both of our dogs decided to leap out of the back of the truck and run back into the house through the open back door. Mom told me to wait here as she, Coreen and Lisa went back inside to fetch the dogs.

Standing nervously by the side of the truck I saw the back door slam shut the moment everyone was inside. Had I been thinking clearer, I would have suggested that we brace every door and window in the house with something before they went back in! As I was staring intently at the house, I was taken by surprise as a large rock hit me square in the back, knocking me to the ground. I looked around, but didn't see anything unusual – which was more than could be said for my Aunt Pat across the street.

She had been watching our house from afar ever since Cousin Jimmy had returned home and told her what had happened during his visit. Aunt Pat had been noticing the lights going on and off for quite a while and the pickup truck still had not moved so she decided to call the police.

When they arrived, I was back in the house with Coreen, Lisa and my mom, who was tending to the cut on my back caused by the rock, which would later require a total of seven stitches to close.

The two policemen came to the front door, knocking as they entered the hall. The first officer asked if everything was alright. My mom replied by simply pointing to the living room where all our furniture was still floating several feet in the air. Under different circumstances I would have laughed as both officer's jaws dropped open and stayed that way.

As we all stared on in wonder, the furniture began to rise all the way to the ceiling and hovered there while Coreen's stereo belted out Alice Cooper's "We're all crazy!" from upstairs. Apparently it was becoming one of "Enoch's" favorites tunes.

The two cops looked at each other in bewilderment. "I'm sorry ma'am but there's nothing we can do for you but give you an escort out of here."

We gladly accepted his offer and headed outside. One of the policemen pulled his car down the driveway and shined his headlights on the truck as we tried to get it started. At this point the lights in the house started to flash on and off extremely fast, like a strobe light.

As my mom tried the ignition again, the engine thankfully started but now the gearshift wouldn't move. Mom struggled desperately until she finally was able to put it in reverse and back out of the driveway and onto the road. We then proceeded down the street with one police car out in front and the other pulling up the rear.

We made a quick stop in front of Aunt Pat's house to drop off Lisa. As Aunt Pat reached to open the passenger door, it flew open by itself, knocking her to the ground. Lisa jumped out of the truck and ran into the house, never looking back. Aunt Pat got to her feet and shouted, "What's going on now?" My mom shook her head and said' "I'll call you later, we've to get out of here now!" as we started down the road again.

After traveling only a few hundred feet, the locks began to pop up and down again and the window cranks started to spin. The truck was rocking from side to side so violently that I could hear the broken glass sifting back and forth in the door wells like a salt shaker.

Looking around, I saw that the police cars were also going though the same thing, rocking back and forth, making it hard for the officers stay on the road. The rocking effect continued for nearly half a mile before gradually fading until we were finally back in control of our vehicles.

CHAPTER EIGHT

OUR NEW HOUSE

Two days later we found ourselves moving into our new home – well new to us anyway. The house itself was actually quite old and in pretty rough shape but it had a couple of great features.

First off, it was only two houses away from my friend Mike Burke who I had known since kindergarten. We had gone through school and cub scouts together and we always had a great time even if we were just hanging out.

The second feature of course was – no ghosts. Something most people would take for granted of course, but for us it was a welcome change.

There were still a number of things that we needed to get from the old house so my mother decided to hire a local guy named Steve Kemple, to assist with the remainder of the move.

After mom and Steve agreed on a plan and a time, we explained everything that had happened to us while we were living in the house so as not to send him into battle without a warning. Steve listened patiently with a slight smile on his face, which turned to outright laughter towards the end.

"You guys are all nuts!" he said mockingly, "There's no such things as ghosts, demons, devils, and all that supernatural B.S. I'll go over there right now to prove to you that there's nothing to be afraid of – it's all in your heads!"

I looked at him calmly and said with a grin, "I'm sure you're right Steve – I guess we just scare easily – a big, strong guy like you should be able to put a ghost like that in its place!"

So my mom and Coreen left in the station wagon with

Steve following, driving my grandmother's car while I went inside the new house to start unpacking.

Mom, Coreen and Steve arrived at our Hurley Pond house around 9:30 that morning. It was unusually warm for January – around 45 degrees, sunny, and so far at least, peaceful and quiet.

Steve backed the station wagon up to the side door that led into the den. He stepped out of the car, looked up at the house and loudly proclaimed, "Here we are Mr. Ghosty man, show me what you've got!"

Pacing back and forth in front of the house, he continued his mocking conversation with no one in particular. He smiled broadly and shouted, "Here ghosty, ghosty, come on out and play ghosty man!"

He looked around for a moment, laughed and shook his head, "Well it looks like there's no ghosts here today; I might as well get to work now." He walked to the back of the station wagon and reached out to open the tailgate. Just before his fingers were able to grab the handle, it flew open, knocking him to ground.

As he laid there in bewilderment starring up at the clear blue sky, Coreen walked over, looked down at him and said, "What was that smart ass, the wind?" Steve glared at her but said nothing. Enjoying herself, Coreen continued, "Quit laying down on the job and give us a hand, we've got work to do."

As they entered the house, they immediately noticed a number of dark smears on most of the walls, apparently made with ash from the fireplace. Most of the marks were random swirls, but as they headed upstairs they were met with Enoch's usual calling card. "YOU ARE ALL DEAD!" was written in big black letters on the wall above the banister.

Mom quickly grabbed a damp rag and began to wipe it off. She glanced at Steve and said, "You guys go ahead and load the car, I'll start cleaning – we can't sell the place with this stuff all over the walls."

Coreen and Steve began moving the remaining boxes to the car, leaving only the heavier furniture behind. The professional movers would have to tackle that when they got there later.

After about an hour, most of the stuff was loaded into the cars.

"All that's left is my stereo, then we're out of here." said Coreen.

As Steve headed back towards the house, he caught some movement out of the corner of his eye. Looking up at the second floor window he saw a face looking at him and waving. He returned inside and asked my mother "Where's Coreen? She was outside with me a minute ago." Immediately Coreen came up behind him and tapped his shoulder, "I'm right here, why?"

Before Steve could answer, the stereo in Coreen's room began playing 'We're All Crazy' at full volume.

Coreen looked at Steve and laughed, "I told you he likes Alice Cooper!"

Her laughter was cut short as the doors upstairs began opening and slamming shut once again. Mom and Coreen knew what to expect next so they quickly grabbed Steve and rushed out of the house before they got locked in again.

Outside, the wind was starting to pick up which was never a good sign.

"Forget the stereo." my mother shouted over the wind, "We'll let the movers get it – if they can. Let's just get in the car and get out of here!"

So mom and Coreen jumped into my grandmother's Duster, which started without a hitch. Steve on the other hand, wasn't so lucky. He turned his key but nothing happened. As he continued to struggle with the ignition, the station wagon began rocking violently from side to side.

At first, Steve had trouble getting out of the car. He tried to open the door, but it wouldn't budge. Mom and Coreen got out of their car and rushed over, trying to open his doors from the outside with no success.

Steve's eyes were beginning to show signs of panic as he clawed desperately at the door handle. Suddenly, all four doors flew open at once and Steve was physically ripped from the driver's seat and thrown to the ground.

At six foot two, and 250 pounds, he was not used to being tossed around like a rag doll, but there he was, struggling against the invisible man as he slowly got dragged over the gravel driveway towards the house.

As he neared the porch, the front door began to open, at which point my mother and Coreen rushed over and grabbed one arm each, trying to prevent him from being pulled into the house.

It took the combined strength of Steve plus both women, to bring him to a stop just outside the front door, which then slowly closed and locked itself with an audible click. Coreen said later that Steve's heart was beating so fast that she could actually hear it just by sitting next to him.

Released by the force that was holding him, Steve quickly got up and staggered back to the station wagon where he sat pouring with sweat even though the temperature was getting close to freezing. After saying a quick prayer, he paused and turned the ignition. This time the car started. He slammed the transmission into gear and rocketed out of the driveway as if Satan himself were chasing him.

My mom got back in her car with Coreen and they stared to back out of the driveway. Looking at the house, Coreen saw a face in one of the dormer windows – a face with no eyes or mouth, just dark spots floating in space. As she turned to tell my mom, they both noticed another wave of rocks rolling toward them, stopping just before the car and forming a wall of gravel that blocked their escape.

Having been through so much lately, my mother was beyond panic or fear, so with a determined look on her face, she angrily jammed her foot down on the gas pedal and drove straight through the wall of stones which rained down on top of her car, but did nothing as far as slowing it down.

Steve was the first to arrive back at our new house, his face literally as white as a ghost. It was obvious that he'd met Enoch and being a wise-ass kid at the time, the first thing I said was "So how'd it go!"

He got out of the car, still shaking slightly and snarled, "Go screw yourself." as he entered the house, grabbed a beer from the fridge and drained it in about two seconds, then reached for another one.

As Steve was finishing his second beer, my mom and Coreen arrived. Mom grabbed a beer for herself and then handed a new one to Steve. "So do you still think we're all liars?" she asked.

"I swear that I will never doubt you again." he said solemnly with a new found appreciation for the paranormal.

CHAPTER NINE

THE TERROR RETURNS

Aftter about a year of uneventful living in our new house, things were about to take a change for the worse yet again.

The summer of 1980 was rapidly drawing to a close and the new school year had just begun. Each morning on my way to the bus stop I would stop by my friend Mike's house, say hi to his mom and then off to school we'd go. As I look back at those happier days I realize now how irreplaceable they would become.

As a few more weeks passed and the trees began to change their color, our favorite time of year was soon to begin – Halloween. Now at the age of twelve, Mike and I could usually be found discussing one of our favorite topics: the various horror and sci-fi movies of the day such as *Star Wars*, *Friday the 13th*, *Dawn of The Dead*, etcetera. This day however, Mike and I were taking our normal walk to the bus stop but instead of talking about movies, we were discussing what we were going to be for Halloween. As we were talking, the climate began to change, going from a mostly sunny morning to a dark and dismal gray.

The wind picked up and the dead but colorful leaves began to swirl and mimic small tornadoes that seemed to follow Mike and I most of the way to the bus stop. Once onboard the bus, we could overhear some of the older kids talking about what they were going to do on mischief night, which was only a couple of days away.

Mike turned to me and said "You know what you should be for Halloween this year? You should do that mummy costume that you did back in Cub Scouts a few years ago. You remember that? You actually won the award for best costume!" Mike laughed.

I looked over and said "Yea, but I had a lot of help from my father and I don't think that I could pull it off as well as he did."

Once the school day had ended, Mike and I caught our bus and began our trek back home as it started to pour with thunder and lightning not far behind.

We ran home as fast as we could trying to stay dry or at least not get struck by lightning. As we neared our homes and started to go our separate ways we heard a loud, sharp bang.

We knew that it wasn't thunder, it sounded more like an M-80 or a shotgun blast and seemed to come from a nearby house – Mr. Sterling's place. Mike and I quickly ran to the front door and knocked. We waited a minute or two and when no one answered we tried the door knob. It was locked. We then ran around to the side of the house and found that door to be unlocked so we entered. Once inside I called out "Mr. Sterling, Mr. Sterling!" but there was no answer. We searched the downstairs finding nothing but noticing that the house was strangely and meticulously neat and in order, almost to the point of being sterile.

Mike and I then made our way upstairs. We searched the first room, nothing. Then as we entered the master bedroom; there on the floor, was a pair of legs sticking out past the edge of the bed. It was Mr. Sterling.

His legs were shaking uncontrollably. The heels of his shoes were making an erratic tapping noise on the floor and then suddenly, all was silent except for the deluge of rain and wind occurring right outside the window.

Mike and I looked at the blood splattered wall behind his bed and it was obvious what had occurred; a suicide. Blood was still dripping from the ceiling and running down the walls. The room still smelled of gunpowder. As we looked over the rest of the body we saw that the self inflicted shotgun blast had resulted in a massive, and obviously fatal head wound. His left eye was laying on his cheek and small streams of blood were oozing from his now slightly exposed eye socket. Flashes of lighting helped illuminate and punctuate the already far too gruesome scene.

"We'd better get some help." Mike said and quickly ran down the stairs and headed out the door with myself not far behind. Upon returning to his house, we quickly phoned for an ambulance.

By now the storm was going at full tilt. Mike and I were watching from his front porch as the paramedics loaded the lifeless body of Mr. Sterling into the back of the ambulance.

As they pulled away, a huge bolt of lightning flashed and was immediately followed by a loud crash of thunder as the house shook and all the lights dimmed and flickered.

I looked over at Mike and said "Well, you and I sure have had one hell of a day so far huh?"

Mike looked at me and said "Yea, but not nearly as bad as the one Mr. Sterling just had."

Then with another flash of lighting the power went out completely. Taking that as my cue to leave, I quickly said my good-byes and ran out the front door through sheets of driving wind and rain to arrive at my house less than 100 yards away.

I called out to see if my sister was home and got no answer. My mother was still at work and said that she probably wouldn't be home until around midnight. I read my usual note from her which was left on the refrigerator.

It stated "Darren I'll be working late tonight. Remember to do your chores and homework. See you in the morning. Love mom." At the bottom of every note she would always write, "PS I love you."

At the time, I remember thinking how mushy and corny that always sounded, but as I grew older, I would miss these notes most of all. It was the little things in life that sometimes carried the greatest meaning.

For the next couple of hours, the power continued its struggle to come back on. As I watched the lights flicker on and off I started to think in the back of my mind, but never aloud, about the one thing that bothered me the most about living in our house on Hurley Pond Road – the feeling that you were always being watched. Then I started remembering how all the lights in the house were going on and off the last night we were there. This brief trip down memory lane coupled with the current thunderstorm and flickering lights was enough to sends shivers down my spine.

I quickly snapped out of it and started looking around for a flashlight or maybe some candles. Fortunately the junk drawer contained one flashlight and three long dinner candles. As usual the flashlight didn't seem to work when I needed it the most so I began to light the candles by using the burner on the stove. A particularly close lightning strike lit up the entire house and was once again followed by a loud crash of thunder. The lights that had been flickering now seemed to be out indefinitely.

Suddenly the front door flew open with a loud slam. It was Coreen. "What's up?" she asked as she walked past, probably noticing the startled look on my face.

"You're not going to believe what happened today."

"Oh yea, what's that?" she replied rather indifferently.

"Mr. Sterling killed himself this afternoon."

"No way! Where?" She asked, suddenly interested.

"Right next door." I replied. "Mike and I heard the shot and ran inside and found him laying there on the floor of his bedroom. You're lucky you weren't here to see him in that condition Coreen."

"Are you okay?" she asked with genuine concern.

"I'm fine. It's just kinda weird to kill yourself right before Halloween."

"Kind of adds to the holiday doesn't it?" was my sister's attempt at a morbid joke.

"It sure does." I said rather dejectedly.

Coreen quickly changed the subject by saying "How about this storm? It's really something isn't it? It's supposed to go on like this until late in the evening and there are flash flood warnings in effect all over the place."

I just nodded in agreement.

"By the way, my boyfriend is coming over in about an hour so try not to bother us."

I agreed and retreated to my bedroom. After a couple of hours, the power finally came back on and stayed on. It was now close to nine o'clock.

I was in my room intending to work on some algebra homework but instead I found myself gazing out the window thinking about what had happened to Mr. Sterling. He always seemed to be such a nice guy. When we moved into this house he was the first one to come over and introduce himself. He handed my mother a bottle of wine and welcomed us to the neighborhood. He had this Bing Crosby kind of personality about him and there in an instant, I saw him lying on the floor in a puddle of blood.

After a few moments I suddenly realized that Coreen was calling me from the living room. Her boyfriend Jeff had arrived.

"Hey we're getting pizza, you want some?"

I nodded yes.

She looked at me and said "Are you sure you're okay?"

"I'm fine, just tired." was all I could muster.

Coreen and Jeff headed out to pick up the food and I stood in the doorway to see them off. In the distance you could hear kids laughing and screaming, your typical pre-Halloween shenanigans.

I closed the door and made my way back through the living room and into the kitchen. As I crossed the threshold leading to my bedroom, the lights in the kitchen began to flicker on and off again. I shrugged it off as being yet another series of power problems due to the storm. I made my way over to my desk and just as I was about to sit down, SLAM! The front door swung wide open followed by a cold blast of air which blew throughout the entire house.

I ran to the living room to close the door when all the lights suddenly went out. As I shut the front door, I turned to my left and right and noticed that both neighbor's house lights were still on. I started to get an uneasy feeling that something was wrong, very wrong.

The lights suddenly came back on as I returned to the kitchen and started to layout some dinner plates and glasses. In the back of my mind all I could think about was our old house. This was all too familiar. I was hoping that it wouldn't be anything like last year and we'd finally be able to get some peace and quiet.

I left everything out for Coreen and Jeff and decided to wait in the living room and watch TV until they returned.

Soon after, the front door opened followed closely by Coreen, Jeff and the smell of piping hot pizza which quickly filled our small house.

We promptly gobbled down dinner in record time, after which Coreen and Jeff proceeded to take over the living room. I decided to go to bed but just as I was beginning to nod out, I heard a loud scream and the sound of breaking glass. The scream came from Coreen, but the breaking glass sounded like it came from the basement. The noise was followed by additional crashing sounds also emanating from the basement.

Our first thought was that someone must have entered the basement through the outside door in an effort to scare us.

Jeff asked Coreen and I, to stay put, saying that he was

going outside to surprise whoever might be down there. I, on the other hand already knew who was down there. But how could it possibly have traveled this amount of distance and have the strength to do what was now transpiring?

Jeff ran out the back door, towards the large metal doors that secured the basement. He saw that they were still locked and the chain was lying undistributed. Then the door began to jiggle as if someone was trying to get out.

Suddenly the door that led from the basement to the kitchen began to slowly open. Coreen noticed it first and ran quickly to try and shut it but was unable to.

"Darren, help me, help me!" she screamed.

I ran over and threw my full weight up against the door which thankfully succeeded in closing it. I then slid the deadbolt over, locking in whatever was down there. By now Jeff had returned from outside and was standing right next to us.

He looked at Coreen and I said, "I think we're all in for a bit of trouble."

In that instant, the lights went out yet again. As we stood helplessly in the dark we heard a noise. Quiet and far off at first, it sounded like someone clapping. It slowly grew louder until it was as if someone were standing right next to you applauding loudly at a concert.

Suddenly the mysterious clapping stopped and the lights came back on. The next sound was all too familiar. It was the sound of all the doors in the house self-locking. I ran to my bedroom to see if we might be able to escape from one of my windows. It was large enough for us to fit through and the jump down to the ground wasn't high at all. I pulled the curtains back and lifted the window open rather easily. I called for Coreen and Jeff.

As they entered the room Coreen pointed and yelled "Darren look out!"

SLAM! The window shut just missing my fingers.

Off in the distance you could hear a humming noise. It was mom's truck. She had just pulled in the driveway. Coreen ran to greet her at the front door and thankfully, it opened easily. Jeff soon joined her by her side.

I sat back down at my desk and a great feeling of ease washed over me. Things were going to be alright. Mom was home.

Before I joined them in the living room, I turned to glance out the window that had nearly broken all my fingers. There starring back at me was the ghostly silhouette of a man, almost faceless. It seemed to be shaking its head back and forth as it slowly disappeared.

CHAPTER TEN

THE BREAK-IN

O ur old house on Hurley Pond Road sat dormant for several weeks after we moved out.

Unfortunately, my cousin Lisa thought that it would be a great idea to tell some of her friends about what had transpired there. So she recounted, with more than a little exaggeration, some of the more disturbing incidents to an audience of wide eyed local kids who reacted with amazement and fear as her tale unfolded.

However, one of the older boys, Sam Desarno, thought that the whole thing was a complete load of crap, but he kept his thoughts to himself until later that day when he met up with his friend, George Thompson.

"You wouldn't believe it." he said. "They all stood around eating this stuff up! Now they want to hold a séance, to communicate with the spirits!" Sam told George laughingly. "Hey, let's sneak in there tonight and set up some 'surprises', we'll scare the hell out of everybody!"

So the two friends wrote down a list of stuff that they would need in order to pull it off and after a couple of hours, they made their way to the back door of our old house which of course was locked. They walked around the structure trying all the other doors and windows but found them to be locked as well.

Losing patience, Sam grabbed a large piece of slate from the border of the fish pond and used it to smash one of the basement windows. The two boys then picked away the sharp fragments of glass and proceeded to crawl through the opening. Once inside George found a seemingly non-functioning light switch before realizing that the power to the house must have been turned off. He grabbed a lighter from his pocket and used its flickering flame to guide them through the long, dark basement to the stairway.

On the way, the two boys horsed around with each other, pushing and shoving, occasionally shouting, "Run, they're coming to get you!" which continued till they reached the top of the stairs. George turned the doorknob and announced "Let there be light!" as he flung the door open allowing the afternoon sun to flood the darkened staircase.

The day was still young and the two of them had plenty of time to execute their plan.

First, they tied a piece of fishing line to the swinging door which led from the kitchen to the dinning room. The other end of the line was attached to the dinning room chandelier, so that each time the swinging door would open or close, the chandelier would move.

Next, they hid a bowling ball in one of the upstairs closets and attached a trip line to the door. They carefully ran the line down the stairs and across the first step, fastening it in such a way that anyone who tried to go upstairs would set off the trip line which would then open the closet door causing the bowling ball to roll down the stairs.

They even went so far as to get some bed sheets and cut eye holes in them, planning to hide in a closet and jump out at the most opportune moment. This, they agreed, would be the grand finale.

The sun was beginning to set when Sam and George finally left the house, confident that they were going to scare the pants off the other kids at the séance that night. As they were walking back through the fields on their way home, Sam stopped suddenly and asked George, "You don't actually believe in ghosts and all that stuff do you?"

George turned to Sam and said "I'll tell you what; I was in that house one night with my brother, just sitting on the sofa watching TV, when something punched me from underneath the cushions. Whatever it was hit me so hard that I fell on the floor and could hardly breathe."

Sam looked at his friend quizzically but said nothing.

George continued, "And that's not all, later that night when we were back at my house, my brother and I were in the basement just talking and joking around, when all of a sudden the power tools came on by themselves. And oh, by the way, the tools weren't even plugged in!"

Sam responded "No way George, that's impossible. You're not gonna get me to believe that! I'm not doubting you or anything but it's just something that I would have to see to believe!"

George looked at Sam and said, "Maybe tonight's the night!" They both laughed and went their separate ways. George yelled out to Sam as he departed, "See ya around eight o'clock!"

As the clock struck eight, Sam's doorbell rang. It was George on time as usual. "Where will everyone be meeting?" asked Sam.

"We're set to meet in the open field just behind the Fitzgerald place." replied George. So off they went, planning the night's activities.

George said, "I think we should make the chandelier move first, that will weed out the chickens, then I'll go hide in the downstairs hall closet until I hear the bowling ball rattle down the stairs. Then, when everybody is running for the door, I'll jump out of the closet with the sheet over my head to block their escape – it'll be the funniest thing ever!"

Sam agreed and couldn't wait to get started.

Within a few minutes Sam and George were greeted by

the rest of the gang, my cousin Lisa, her friends Kim and Terry, and George's brother Rich. Lisa brought the Ouija board and some candles, and everyone carried their own flashlight. There was a palpable aire of excitement as they made the trek through the woods to the old house.

Sam and George played it up as if they hadn't visited the place since the Fitzgeralds moved out. George said "Looks like all the doors are all locked, but look, there's a broken window by the fish pond."

They all made their way through the window and into the basement. George and Sam hung back, letting Lisa lead the way up the staircase.

Upon reaching the top of the stairs they were startled by a loud BANG, BANG, BANG, BANG coming from somewhere within the house.

Terry and Kim yelped in fright but George and Sam recognized the sound as that of the bowling ball bouncing down the stairs – but what they couldn't understand was, who tripped the wire?

For a few moments the group stood in the entrance hall, talking and nervously waving their flashlights around, until George said, "Let's go that way." as he pointed his beam of light towards the swinging door.

"Okay." replied Lisa as she pushed the door open. The chandelier did not move. Sam shone his flashlight around the room, looking for the fishing line they had set up, but it was gone. As the beam of light moved around the room he saw the bowling ball on the floor in the corner. Sam and George began to suspect that someone else was already in the house playing a prank on the pranksters! They looked at each other quizzically but said nothing.

Unaware of the prank gone bad, Lisa ordered everyone to sit on the floor, so that they could begin the séance. Kim set her candles around the Ouija board and lit them while Lisa got everyone into position, telling them to join hands and keep silent.

Lisa then placed her fingertips on the outer edges of the planchette and began to ask the typical questions, "If you are here, give us a sign!"

An uneasy silence followed. Sam and George looked at each other sheepishly – they didn't really believe in any of this supernatural nonsense did they? The only reason they were there in the first place was to play a practical joke on the others and since that had somehow been spoiled, they weren't sure what to do next. They waited uncomfortably as Lisa tried again to get the spirit's attention.

"Spirit of the house, give us a sign!" she asked, but again, no response.

Finally Sam broke the silence "Ask your stupid ghost if he likes this sign." as he raised his middle finger in an obscene gesture.

George began to laugh, then Kim joined in. Soon everyone was laughing, not so much at Sam's joke, but as a means to break the silence.

The laughter stopped abruptly as the planchette began to spin out of control. As everyone sat mesmerized, the Ouija board suddenly rose up from the floor and slammed into the ceiling, smashing the plastic pointer into tiny fragments that rained down upon them all.

Now in a complete state of panic, the group scattered, running in different directions. Kim ran out through the basement door, the same way that she had come in but as soon as she crossed the threshold, the door slammed shut behind her knocking her to the bottom of the stairs where she laid unconscious for several minutes.

Lisa, Terry and Rich ran to the front door but were unable to open it. Crying and screaming, they pounded on the door for quite some time before collapsing to the floor, where they huddled together in terror.

Sam and George heard the commotion at the cellar door

and ran to help, but the door wouldn't open. They called out to Kim but there was no answer. Desperate to save their friend, the boys tried to knock the door down but only succeeded in bruising their shoulders.

A few minutes later, Kim regained consciousness. The first thing she tried to do was find her flashlight by feeling around in the pitch black darkness. After failing to find it she tried to stand, but her left leg quickly collapsed followed by a wave of excruciating pain. She realized then that her leg was probably broken. In great pain, she began to crawl along the dark basement floor, feeling her way along the walls like a blind person. She managed to locate the broken window from which they had entered, but the pain in her injured leg prevented her from pulling herself up and climbing out, so she sat there, quiet but terrified, until dawn.

Meanwhile upstairs, Lisa, Terry, Rich, Sam and George were still desperately trying to escape. Sam took off his shirt, wrapped it around his right hand, and tried to punch the glass out of one of the dinning room windows, but his fist bounced off the glass as if it were made out of stone.

As Sam held his aching hand, George located an old wooden chair, which he raised above his head and threw at the window shouting, "Here goes nothing!"

The chair sailed through the air, hit the window and bounced off the glass as if it were a rubber ball. After several more attempts it became obvious that they would not be leaving anytime soon.

That night was one they would never forget. All they could do was huddle together in the dark and wait for help to arrive as the house came to life.

First there was a muffled banging that slowly became louder. As the banging grew in strength all the lights in the house came on at once while the temperature became icy cold.

Sam and George could see their breath as they spoke.

George said in a light whisper "Hey Sam do you believe in ghosts now?"

The banging continued well into the night. Once in a while they could hear voices, some female, some deep and menacing – but always telling them that they were going to die.

Finally morning arrived and as the sun began to break through the windows, all the doors in the house opened at once. In the calm light of dawn, it seemed almost impossible to believe if what had happened to them was real or a dream. Dazed by a night of sheer terror, each of them questioned their own sanity – until they found Kim downstairs. Her bruises and broken leg were all too real to simply explain away.

Nonetheless, all of the individuals involved in this night ended up keeping their experiences secret for most of their adult lives.

CHAPTER ELEVEN

THE NEW RESIDENTS

Billy and Milly Richards were enjoying the mild spring weather as they cruised down the Garden State Parkway in Billy's brand new 1980 Lincoln Continental Mark IV coupe.

Billy was a twenty-nine year old Harvard graduate and a successful investment banker. Milly, his wife of two years, was twenty seven and a legal assistant at a prestigious Manhattan law firm where her father was a partner.

Gliding down the highway at a moderate pace, Billy reached over and turned up the volume on his custom sound system.

"Never can get enough of that Springsteen – right babe?" he shouted over the blaring strains of 'Born to Run'

"You know it honey, he's the boss!" Milly replied smiling. She was especially happy this day as they were en route to their new "country house" along one of the many back roads of central New Jersey.

Though they both worked in midtown Manhattan and owned a large apartment on the Upper East Side, the couple felt that they needed a quiet place where they could escape their busy lives. After spending most of the winter looking at various properties in the suburbs of New Jersey, New York, and Connecticut, they finally settled on a small horse farm located within biking distance of the beach in eastern New Jersey. Being the busy people that they were, they had hired an interior decorator to pick out paint and new furniture to fill the many rooms.

Within a few weeks the happy news arrived informing them that their house has been painted and furnished and the couple would be able to move in at any time.

Milly was especially excited to begin living the country life. "What a great address – Hurley Pond Road – it sounded so… so charming." She said.

"Yeah…" replied Billy. "It's going to be a great place to relax. You know, just sit around with absolutely nothing to do – so peaceful – exactly what we need!"

It was mid afternoon by the time they finally arrived and from the outside, everything looked to be in order. But when they entered through the front door, the first thing they noticed was that the new bedroom set was stacked neatly on top of the dinning room table.

"Well that's just great!" Milly said disgustedly, "They said everything was perfect… perfect my ass!"

Billy looked around scowling, "Where's the phone?"

"It's not hooked up yet!" Milly said, her voice rising in anger. "That's another thing they said they were going to get done!"

They got back into their Lincoln and drove towards town to find a pay phone. Milly vented her frustration to the decorator for nearly fifteen minutes, finally stopping long enough to let him apologize and promise that he'd have some men over there right away.

Feeling slightly better, Billy and Milly drove back to their new house only to find that all their furniture had been returned to its rightful positions. Milly stared dumbfounded at the empty dining room table – there wasn't even a mark on the highly polished finish to suggest that the other stuff was ever there.

Billy ran upstairs to the master bedroom to find his new

Mediterranean style bedroom set arranged perfectly, even the bed sheets were turned down.

More confused than ever, Billy and Milly just looked at each other speechlessly for several minutes until the men sent by the decorator arrived.

The couple apologized to the men and struggled to explain what had happened.

Scratching his head, Billy said, "It must have been a practical joke by some locals – maybe those kids who broke in a few weeks ago…"

Grumbling over the wasted trip, the men left with lots of apologies but no tip.

Although it didn't seem likely that local kids would break in and neatly stack furniture onto the dining room table, then sneak in again and put it all back, but Billy and Milly could think of no other explanation, so they had to accept this implausible scenario as the truth.

Still they both had an uneasy feeling as they began to unpack and settle into their new house. As evening approached, the last thing they were able to finish was organizing the kitchen utensils before turning off the downstairs lights and heading upstairs to bed.

As Milly busied herself in the bathroom, Billy tried to locate his pajamas. "They're up here somewhere." He muttered, as he wandered from room to room. At one point he walked down the hall to check the back bedroom when he noticed that a light was left on downstairs. He went back down and found that the kitchen light was turned on although he was quite certain that he had turned it off earlier. Billy looked around and checked the door locks but saw nothing unusual, so he turned off the light and headed back upstairs.

Billy finally was able to locate his pajamas in the hallway closet and he brought them with him to the bathroom where he changed and got ready for bed. He returned to the master bedroom and lied down on the plush king size mattress, sighing contentedly.

A few moments later Milly came in; "Honey, you forgot to turn off the light in the kitchen."

Billy's head snapped up, "What?" he asked incredulously.

"Oh, that's okay, I went down and shut it off myself." Milly replied.

Without a word, Billy jumped up and rushed out to the hallway to look down the stairwell. There was a faint glow coming from the kitchen again!

Moments later Milly joined him, "That's weird, I swear I just shut it off – I'm absolutely positive…"

"Yeah, never mind – I think there's a problem with the wiring, I'll call an electrician in the morning, for now, let's just leave it on." Billy said, not really believing his own words.

Nevertheless, the couple was tired from a long and stressful day, so just after eight o'clock, they decided to turn out the bedroom lights and try to get some sleep.

By nine o'clock it was apparent that sleep would not be coming anytime soon. The combination of being in a new house and the lack of city sounds, as well as the unfamiliar creeks and groans of an old structure, all prevented them from relaxing enough to sleep – that and the footsteps.

Just after nine o'clock, Billy sat bolt upright on the bed.

"What the heck is that …" Milly's words were cut short by Billy.

"Quiet!" he hissed.

In the silence that followed, they both heard it – the unmistakable sound of footsteps coming up the stairs.

Billy jumped out of bed and turned on the light. He fumbled frantically in the closet and quickly emerged with his wooden baseball bat.

"Who's there!" he shouted.

But there was only silence. Slowly he made his way out of

the bedroom and into the hallway. He reached for the switch on the wall and flipped it, but nothing happened.

Then the footsteps began anew, getting closer this time.

Billy fumbled frantically at the wall and managed to hit another switch which succeeded in turning on the hall lights – but there was nothing. Billy carefully advanced toward the stairwell and peered over it – still nothing.

With Milly following close behind and carrying the flashlight, they slowly crept down the stairs with Billy holding the bat outstretched in front of him with trembling hands. As he reached the bottom of the stairway, he turned on the entry hall light, which also revealed nothing.

After a cautious search of the entire house, Billy and Milly returned to the master bedroom and again, turned out the lights and tried to get some sleep. Milly lied down on the bed and closed her eyes, wondering just what she had gotten herself into while Billy sat in a chair next to the door, listening nervously for the phantom footsteps to begin again, but there was only silence – maddening, deafening, silence.

After hours of tense waiting, mixed with brief moments of uneasy dozing, it was almost a relief when the sound of steady, deliberate footsteps broke the silence.

Billy sprang from his chair to the doorway where he saw a dim, flickering light approaching. He leaped into the hall and slapped the light switch on with his left hand while his right hand clutched the Louisville Slugger. As the light illuminated the hallway, Billy was able to glimpse a shadowy figure coming towards him. Panicking, he swung his bat wildly, connecting to something with a glancing blow.

"Billy you idiot!" Milly screamed as she brought her hand to her forehead, "What the hell's wrong with you!"

"Oh my God… I'm sorry honey, I thought…" Billy stammered, "What are you doing out here anyway?" he asked.

"I just went to get a towel from the closet." Milly replied, wincing as she poked tenderly at the rapidly swelling knot on her forehead.

"Okay honey, I'll go down to the kitchen and get some ice." as he headed toward the stairway.

Upon reaching the top of the stairs, he suddenly flew forward, as if pushed hard from behind. He fell headfirst four or five steps before landing on his forearms which he held out instinctively in front of him, bracing for impact. He rolled awkwardly down the remaining steps until he hit the dining room floor.

Milly rushed down after him "Are you alright?" she cried, "What happened?"

"I... I don't know, something pushed me from behind... am I bleeding?" Billy asked.

"You've got some cuts on your head – how do your arms feel?" Milly replied.

"I don't think they're broken..." Billy said as he looked around nervously, "Now lets get the heck out of here!"

Waking up to the sound of her doorbell, Aunt Pat glanced at the clock. Who could it possibly be at six o'clock in the morning she thought as she put on her robe and headed toward the foyer. Opening the front door she saw a young couple that has apparently been in an auto accident. The gentleman had cuts and bruises on his face and forearms while the lady has a large ugly swelling on her forehead.

"Come in, come in, are you hurt?" Pat asked as she ushered the couple into the family room.

"We're sorry to bother you ma'am, my name is Billy Richards and this is my wife Milly – we just moved into the old Fitzgerald house and, well..." Billy's words trailed off as he looked uncomfortably at the ground.

"Oh… so you're the ones." Aunt Pat said ominously, "Well, all I can say is – you bought yourself one hell of a house!" She motioned toward the couch, "Come sit down, I'll make some coffee and tell you a little something about your new home."

Thirty minutes later Billy and Milly Richards thanked Aunt Pat and returned to their house. Less than an hour later, the young couple emerged carrying several suitcases, which they packed into the spacious trunk of their Lincoln. They both got in their car and drove away, never to return. A few days later, when asked by the real estate agent what to do with the furniture Billy replied "Sell it, give it to charity, burn it – I don't care, just get rid of it – all of it, I don't ever want to hear the name Hurley Pond again!"

The Chase family was sitting around the living room watching TV and catching up with the events of the last few days. The hot topic that night, of course, was the young couple who had just abandoned the 'Fitzgerald place' after only one night.

"They really looked banged up." Aunt Pat said, "It's no wonder they refused to stay another night!"

"Well, old Frank Sampson will have to find another buyer now – and probably from out of state." Egon said. "Nobody around here will touch the place."

"Yeah, that house is pretty freaky!" Tammy exclaimed. "Remember that time…" but she was abruptly cut off by her mother.

"That's enough Tammy, you'll give your little sister nightmares – let's just be thankful nobody got hurt."

Pat managed to steer the conversation to more pleasant

topics until ten o'clock when she announced, "Okay kids, time for bed – you've got school tomorrow…"

"With all the moaning and groaning – you'd think that I'd just asked them to pull out their own teeth." Pat thought. The kids slowly made their way upstairs to get ready for bed.

Pat returned to the living room to tidy up, glancing disdainfully at the stuffed deer head hanging over the fireplace as she picked up the empty soda cans and food wrappers. She cursed the day that Egon found that monstrosity at a local garage sale and insisted on hanging it in their living room. Of course the kids loved it and immediately started calling it "Bambi" – much to Pat's dismay, as that was one of her favorite movies when she was younger.

The children however, had no such sentimental feelings. Jimmy was already in the habit of hanging his baseball cap on one of the antlers and when little Jamie-Ann asked how it died, Tammy joked, "He ate grandma's fruitcake from last Christmas!"

If nothing else, it was definitely too dusty and might even have fleas, mused Pat and she resolved to get the hideous thing out of her house by spring. As she wandered around the living room cleaning, she noticed something odd – the eyes of the deer seemed to follow her as she moved. No matter which side of the room she was on, the deer's dead, soulless, glass eyes seemed to be staring directly at her. It must be a trick of the dim lighting she thought, but her heart was beating a little faster as she quickly exited the room.

Whistling a little nervously, she walked across the street to the barn to check on the horses. This was Pat's favorite time of the evening – no matter how hectic her day had been, the presence of the animals always seemed to have a calming effect. But tonight the two horses – Clover, a spotted chestnut mare, and Shamrock, a handsome former show-horse – seemed agitated, snorting and shaking their heads restlessly.

Pat approached the animals slowly, talking quietly until

she was close enough to reach out and rub their noses. With soothing words and a few apples, she quieted the big animals and moved on to the dogs – Shamus, a frisky Golden Retriever, and Daisy, a more sedate Basset Hound – making sure they had enough food and water, before turning out the light and walking back across the street.

Once inside her house, she headed over to the kitchen and began to wash the few dishes that were left in the sink. Though tired, she prided herself on never leaving dirty dishes for the morning. As she rinsed the silverware, the light above the sink began to turn on and off – not a rapid blinking like an electrical problem, but more of a slow, steady on/off sequence that continued for several minutes.

A little nervously she called out for Egon, "Honey, could you come here a minute, I think there's something wrong with the kitchen lights."

A few moments later Egon appeared along with Tammy, who was carrying her young sister Jamie-Ann in her arms. By this time, the light has stopped blinking and was burning steadily once again.

Pat sighed in exasperation, "I'm telling you, just a minute ago it was turning on and ..." But she was interrupted by a creaking noise as one of the cabinet doors slowly swung open, revealing stacks of dinner plates and coffee cups. As they all looked on in disbelief, the plates and cups began to smash to pieces, as if struck by an invisible hammer.

For two long minutes the air was filled with the sound of smashing glassware as one by one, the other cabinet doors opened and the plates and glasses inside began to shatter as well.

Pat, Egon and the girls stood frozen in place for several moments, paralyzed with fear until little Jamie-Ann started crying, snapping Pat out of her daze.

"Tammy, you and your sister get out of here – there's glass all over the place and you're running around barefoot!"

shouted Pat as he looked around wildly, "Come on, get your coats on and let's all get the heck out of here!"

Tammy and Jamie were hurrying along the counter toward the doorway, but as they passed the last cabinet, Jamie's hand reached out to retrieve the only remaining piece of unbroken china.

"Don't touch that!", Tammy yelled, trying to swat Jamie's hand away, but it was too late. As Jamie-Ann's searching fingers approach the cabinet, a jagged shard of glass flew off the shelf, slicing her left forearm from the palm all the way to the elbow.

Jamie-Ann let out a blood-curdling scream as blood begins to spurt from the massive wound. Tammy stood wide-eyed and pale, unable to move as her yellow terry cloth robe rapidly turned crimson. Egon grabbed some towels while Pat tried to calm the screaming child. Using a half dozen dish towels, Egon was finally able to control the bleeding. Unfortunately he knew that they needed to get her to a hospital quickly for stitches.

Meanwhile, all the commotion brought the remaining children – Jimmy, Lisa and Egon Jr., running downstairs where they all jostled into one another at the kitchen door. Trying to get a good view, but too scared to go in, there was a collective gasp as they took in the destruction before them. Not only the heaps of broken china that had spilled from the cabinets and littered the floor, but also the bloodstains that seemed to be everywhere – on the floor, the countertops and all of the previously white dish towels.

"What happened!" exclaimed Jimmy, but his question went unanswered as Egon and Pat bundled Jamie-Ann in a warm blanket.

"I'll bring her to the emergency room," Egon shouted. "Pat, you get the kids packed up and over to the Fitzgerald's new house. We're not staying here tonight!"

The next day, Egon called old Frank Sampson at his real estate office. "Hi Frank, this is Egon Chase, you probably know our friends, the Fitzgeralds – they just sold their place on Hurley Pond Road a few weeks ago. "Well, anyway, we're looking to move too and wondered if you could list our house…"

Six weeks later, the Chase family was living happily in rural New York State, on a farm just outside of Cooperstown. They would never return to Hurley Pond Road again.

CHAPTER TWELVE

DEATH OF A FRIEND

O n one particularly hot and muggy afternoon in the Summer of 1983 my good friend Jimmy Spense stopped over driving his 1968 Pontiac Tempest which we had affectionately nicknamed the Batmobile. He pulled into my driveway around one o'clock in the afternoon with three other occupants; Terry Strawberinger, Rich Archer and Glenn Felise. We all headed into my garage to hang out while we thought up something to do.

We broke out some beers and started to talk about going to see a movie later that night when Jimmy suddenly perked up and said, with just a hint of sarcasm in his voice, "Hey Darren, why don't you tell us about that house you used to live in on Hurley Pond Road again." Jimmy was a pretty tough young guy and had always doubted any story related to the supernatural. He continued, "No offense Darren, but it's hard to believe all the stuff you say happened, I mean, come on – furniture hanging in the air, waves of rocks in the driveway, doors slamming on their own – none of that could have happened and you know it!"

"Well what if I could prove it to you." I replied.

To which Terry followed with, "Jimmy, how 'bout you drive us all over there? We'll park down the road a bit and use the Ouija board. Darren knows how to use it." I agreed but warned everyone that the Ouija board was not a toy and whatever happened would have to stay between us.

We all piled into Jimmy's Batmobile and headed off, stopping at Terry's house which was just a few hundred yards down the street. She ran inside and returned with her mother's Ouija board. Within a few minutes we were parked on the side of Hurley Pond road, about fifty yards from my old house.

Jimmy and I were in the front seat with the board while Terry, Rich and Glenn sat in the backseat. I placed the golden heart pointer on the board's flat surface while Jimmy and I held the edges - Jimmy asked the questions. He started with a simple one, "Is anybody out there?" he asked skeptically. Glenn and I closed our eyes and relaxed, trying to let the spirits control our hands but there was no response. Jimmy continued, "Is there anyone named Enoch here?" and again there was no response from the board.

Jimmy was exasperated, "Come on guys lets get out of here, this is bullshit!"

I turned to Glen who was in the backseat and said "You try it with me, just relax and let the heart move on its own." I started by saying "Enoch, if you can hear me then give me a sign." The heart didn't move, but within seconds the sunny skies began to turn cloudy and the wind started to pick up.

"Big deal," said Rich "The weatherman mentioned that there might be rain today..." but he was interrupted by Glen.

"Enoch, I ask you one more time, give us a sign, NOW!"

At that instant the window cranks started to spin, opening all four windows at once. Rich just sat there frozen with his jaw hanging open, while Terry began to panic.

"I knew it – I knew this place was messed up, let's get out of here NOW!" Terry shouted, her eyes wide with fear. But immediately the car began to rock from side to side violently.

Rich was pale and visibly shaking, "Okay, okay, I believe you now, get it to stop!" he shouted, but all I could do was shrug my shoulders and say "I can't."

After about a minute the rocking had died down and it looked as if it were going to be over soon, but suddenly all four car doors flew open. Terry screamed while Jimmy turned the ignition and thankfully, the car started. We managed to pull the doors closed and Jimmy put his car in gear and started to pull away, but within a few yards, the rocking returned accompanied by a loud banging noise, as if several hammers were pounding on the outside of his vehicle. Jimmy hit the brakes and as the car screeched to a halt, all four side windows shattered and exploded outward, sending shards of glass all over the road but nothing at all inside the car.

"The hell with this!" Jimmy exclaimed as he hit the gas hard. The car lurched forward, picking up speed as we approached a small bridge that spanned a creek. As soon as we reached the top of the bridge the rocking and banging ceased as suddenly as it began. We traveled another hundred yards or so before Jimmy pulled his car over and stopped.

Jimmy turned to me and smiled for the first time that afternoon. "That was the coolest thing I've ever seen Darren!" and began to laugh.

"Screw that!" Glenn exclaimed, "Let's go get a case of beer – I'm buying!" He was laughing, but his right hand was still clenched to the door handle with a white-knuckled death grip.

The events of that afternoon would stay secret among us until one year later when I received a phone call from Jim. "Are you going to be able to make it to the party this Friday night?" he asked.

"I wouldn't miss it for the world." I replied

"Great, we can't wait to see you." Jimmy said. "I apologize Darren but, I need to cut this conversation short. I've got this really terrible headache and I need to get some sleep."

"No problem, I'll call you tomorrow after I get off work." These were the last words that I would ever get to say to him.

Upon returning home from work I found both Glen and Rich sitting on the front porch of my house. As I walked up the driveway my mom came out the front door and brought me aside. "We need to talk Darren."

She quickly whisked me past my friends and into our house, asking me to take a seat in the kitchen.

"I don't know how to say this so here it goes," She paused for a moment while I continued to sit in silence.

"At some point during the night last night your friend Jimmy suffered a massive brain aneurism and is now in intensive care on life support. His family is requesting your presence by his side. They think that he may pass tonight."

As I sat numbly in the chair, my eyes drifted off of my mother's face and settled onto a photograph which was stuck to the refrigerator door. It was a photo of Jimmy and I from the previous summer – the two of us appeared to be laughing at a joke. My eyes began to fill with tears as the gravity of the situation set in.

When I arrived at the hospital I could not prepare myself for what I was about to witness. I made my way around the curtain which surrounded Jimmy's bed and there, lying motionless was Jim. This once vibrant, intelligent, funny and kind person was now reduced to being kept alive solely by machines. The noises in the room added to the dire situation. The beeping of the heart monitor, the dripping of the intravenous unit, and the rise and fall of Jimmy's chest which was mechanically controlled by a respirator with its deep hallow sucking sound. These noises still echo in my memory to this very day. As I continued to look down at him, I noticed that his eyes were slightly open but all you could see were the whites. There were still remnants of what appeared to be dried blood in his ears and nasal passages. I knew right then that he wouldn't be coming back.

I ended up spending the next four days at his bedside only going home to shower and fill my mother in on the latest news. On the fourth day, Jimmy's parents finally decided to release him from this grey area between life and death.

A few hours later a priest showed up to gave Jimmy his

last rites. After the priest had recited his final prayer, the doctor set about turning off his life support. Jimmy died immediately. That's when the tears that I had been keeping pent up inside finally fell. His death affected me far more so than any other loss that I had experienced so far.

After his funeral I consoled in my mother who was acting more like my best friend at the time and told her that Jim's death was really bothering me. My dreams were not dreams anymore at that point – they were nightmares. Everything from the events at our old house right down to the sucking sound of the respirator all haunted me greatly.

My mom listened patiently to everything that I had to say. She gave me something to hold onto by saying "That's because he died so young and of natural causes – it always seems more tragic when the good ones are taken before their time".

Wise words. Over the next few years, their meaning would be driven home time and time again.

DOWN BY THE RIVER

For the next year or so we were able to enjoy a normal suburban life without blinking lights, slamming doors, ominous writing, flying rocks, etcetera. My friend Mike Burke used to stop over almost daily and soon I began to tell him everything that happened to my family while we were living at the Hurley Pond house. Mike was fascinated by the supernatural and never once laughed or called me crazy, but instead just listened intently to every word. "I wish I could have seen that!" he would often say, not realizing that he would soon have a few supernatural experiences of his own.

On one late summer afternoon Mike and a mutual friend, Eric Boyd were riding their bicycles past my old house which was up for sale yet again when they happened to notice that the hanging for-sale sign had fallen off of its metal post and was lying face down on the grass. In a simple effort to assist whoever was trying to sell the house, Mike and Eric decided to drop their bikes and reset the sign onto it's post. It took the strength of both of them to lift the heavy metal sign back over the two hooks that held it in place.

After the simple fix they remounted their bicycles and started to leave. Mike was out in front and as he got to the stop sign at the top of the hill he looked back over his shoulder to see where Eric was. Mike laughed to himself as he saw Eric huffing, puffing and sweating profusely as he pedaled hard to make it up the hill but what Mike noticed over Eric's shoulder stopped his laughter immediately. The heavy metal for-sale sign which took two people to lift over the hooks was off of it's hinges once again, lying face down on the lawn. This was exceptionally odd since it was a completely windless day so there was no chance that it could have blown off.

Aware of the history of the house, both boys stood frozen for a minute, the hairs on the back of their necks standing straight up. They looked at each other with eyes wide before pedaling away as fast as they could. Going back to re-hang the sign for a second time was not an option.

A few days later Mike stopped over at my house and happened to mention the whole for-sale sign story to my mother.

She replied, "You think that's something, wait till you see this." She sat down at the kitchen table along with Coreen, Mike and myself and said, "Don't tell anyone about what you're about to see. We'll just call it an old Irish magic trick."

She placed an empty crystal glass on the table, then took off her old wedding band which she still wore, along with the gold necklace that hung around her neck. She threaded the ring through the necklace and suspended it directly over the glass with the ring hanging just below the rim.

"You can ask a total of five questions about the future and the ring will answer by tapping the glass once for 'Yes' and twice for 'No'."

"I'll start first" she said and asked, "Will I ever live on a farm with horses again?" The ring tapped the glass once – 'Yes'.

I asked the next question, "Will I graduate from high school?" The ring tapped the glass twice – 'No'.

Mike laughed and said "I could have told you that." but

I continued...

"Will I ever break a bone?" This time the glass answered 'Yes'.

Then my mom interrupted, "Let Mike have a turn."

Mike asked, "Will I be successful in my career?" The glass answered 'Yes'.

I asked my mom if I'd be able to ask one more question. "Okay, but make it quick." was her reply.

So with thoughts of my old friend Jimmy Spense still stuck in my mind I asked, "Will I lose anyone else who's close to me this year?"

Immediately my mom shot me a steely eyed glance that pretty much said "You shouldn't ask it things like that."

The ring struck the glass once – the answer, much to my dismay was yes.

I looked at my mom and quickly apologized, "I'm sorry mom, who do you think it could be?"

As she put the ring back on her finger and the chain back around her neck she said, "I have no idea. Is anyone close to you very ill right now?"

I replied "No."

"Then your guess is as good as mine." was my mother's only response.

Despite this slightly ominous event, life in the 'new' house continued to be relatively quiet and uneventful ever since the incident on the day that Mr. Sterling committed suicide. Coreen and I continued to attend school, fought and argued with each other as brothers and sisters do, but never anything serious – the events of the last few years had actually brought us closer.

I had pretty much forgotten about the predictions made by the ring and glass until one day in the spring of 1984.

I was anxious to try out the new dirt bike that I had just purchased, so I brought it out to a nearby field where some of the other neighborhood kids and I had laid out a track that wound through the woods for about half a mile.

The first part of the course was a long dirt road that cut across an open field, then up a series of hills, finally twisting back through a thick woods. I knew the trail like the back of my hand and decided to open the throttle wide to see what my new motorcycle could do.

Flying down the bumpy dirt path in fifth gear, I pushed the bike until it would go no faster. I mounted the top of a hill at full speed, coming off the ground and sailing about 20 feet in the air. I landed perfectly, with the back wheel coming down straight but not too hard. I had lost very little speed on the jump and continued barreling down the path as fast as I could go – that's when I saw it but it was already too late. A steel guy-wire cable leading from an old telephone pole to the ground right in front of me.

I reacted primarily out of instinct, letting go of the handlebars and raising my right arm to block the cable. It's probably what kept me from losing my head – literally.

Instead, I woke up in the hospital with a pain in my back and a large cast over my entire right arm from shoulder to wrist. I had broken my wrist, elbow, upper arm and shoulder in addition to 26 of the 28 bones in my right hand. Still the doctors called me "lucky". I would spend the next two weeks trapped in my hospital bed, thinking about how "lucky" I was.

After I had healed enough to leave, I returned home, but still had to spend a great deal of time in bed with my arm elevated. On my first day back, Mike stopped by and said, in his typical fashion, "Hey Evel Knievel, I patched up your bike up so let's ride – or are you too scared?"

We both laughed and I replied "In a couple of days I'll be back on my feet and I'll ride your sorry ass into the dirt!"

Mike said, "Yea we'll see about that, but in the meantime, there's this old abandoned house down by the river that everybody says is haunted – I say that you and I should check it out if you're up for it!"

I quickly agreed. After living in the house on Hurley Pond Road for so many years this house would have to be pretty damn haunted to scare me! So a few minutes later Mike and I were on our way. We found the house in question; a dilapidated old building set far off the road. With its broken windows and peeling paint it certainly looked haunted at least. Mike and I entered through a broken door in the back and took a look around. There wasn't much to see since the house was practically devoid of everything save for some clothing in the closets and of all things, a baby grand piano in the corner of the living room.

I noticed that nearly every door in the house had one of those old-fashioned glass doorknobs on it which might be worth something to someone so Mike and I set about trying to find a screwdriver to unscrew them with. Mike was able to dig up a couple of dull butter knives from underneath one of the kitchen cabinets which actually did the trick. As he began to unscrew one of the knobs I started poking through the closets, checking out some of the moldy, moth eaten clothes that looked as if they had been purchased back in the 1940's.

I picked up a particularly gaudy red dress and held it up to Mike. "This would look good on you." I said, "It really brings out the color of your eyes."

"Yeah, but you've got the legs for it." Mike replied laughingly, "Here's another knife smart-ass, why don't you get to work on that other door." as he slid the second butter knife across the floor to me. I returned the dress to the closet and began removing the knob from the bedroom door, while Mike continued working on the bathroom's.

After a moment, Mike said, "What do you want?"

"I don't want anything, what are you talking about?" I replied.

"You just tapped me on the shoulder, didn't you?"

"I couldn't have," I said, "I'm way the hell over here – just finish getting these knobs off and let's get out of here."

I finished removing the faceplate and the whole assembly fell to the floor with a clang. As I bent down to pick up the pieces, I suddenly noticed a large dead rat behind the door. Apparently it had been dead for quite some time as the skin was dried and stretched tightly over it's small thin bones giving it the appearance of a mummy.

I called Mike over to take a look.

"Wow, that's one big rat," he said. "But take a closer look. Have you ever seen anything like this before?"

Assuming that he was asking a serious question, he managed to draw me in a bit closer before kicking the damn thing directly towards my face which was less that a couple of feet away at that point.

Dodging out of the way in the nick of time, an impromptu, laugh filled soccer match then ensued with the mummified rat acting as the ball.

The game only lasted for a couple of minutes before we got bored and just a little disgusted with our actions. We kicked the rat off to the corner of the room and went back to removing doorknobs.

A few minutes had passed when all of a sudden I heard Mike yell, "Darren!"

I whipped around to see what was wrong and immediately noticed that Mike looked visibly concerned and not at all in a joking mood like he was before.

"Something just slapped me on the back and I could have sworn it was you throwing that rat on me!"

The rat was still laying undisturbed in the corner of the room where we had kicked it previously.

I felt the hairs on the back of my neck begin to rise as they often did when weird things happened. As my gaze slowly changed from Mike's face to just above his left shoulder, I noticed what appeared to be a hand written note on a small piece of old faded legal paper tacked to the wall. Although the paper was obviously very old, the writing looked some-what fresh – "Call Chett Baxter," was all it said.

Of course I knew the story of Chett Baxter from living at my old house. But we were miles from Hurley Pond Road – how did Enoch know I was here? Did he control this house too or did he control me?

I was literally numb with fear as I backed away slowly from the wall.

Mike noticed the terrified look on my face and I of course noticed the terrified look on his, so we both quickly came to the same conclusion – run!

We weren't about to take the slow route of traversing through the rest of the darkened house to locate the door that we had entered through. Instead our focus had turned to a much easier means of escape. The blown out window of the bedroom which we were already in.

I went first, bolting towards the window like a linebacker but right before I reached the exit, I must have stepped on a rotten floorboard and nearly fell through to the basement. The only thing that stopped me was the bulky cast which I still wore.

As luck would have it, I was now trapped in the floor and blocking our only viable means of escape.

Mike rushed over and asked, "Are you all right?"

I replied "Yeah, but I think some of the pins in my arm came loose; I can feel blood in my cast."

As I sat there pinned by the broken floorboards which immobilized me as if I were in a crude bear trap, I suddenly noticed how big, dark and ominous the house began to look. Even though it was early afternoon on a sunny day, most of the windows in the house had been boarded up giving the place a very dark and sinister feel.

As Mike continued to try to pull me out of the broken floor, I also started to notice that there were way too many doors, closets, and other rooms connected to the room we were in, giving me a very vulnerable feeling. I had an image in my head that at any moment we would be set upon from one of the many open doorways by some unimaginable horror.

After more than a few minutes of lifting and pulling, Mike was finally able to help free me from my trap. Without wasting any time, we both jumped out of the narrow window and rolled out onto the front porch. Immediately we were back on our feet and running away from the house as fast as our legs could carry us. We didn't stop running till we hit the street.

Mike looked down at my cast and said "You're bleeding pretty bad, we better get you home."

I kind of knew what must have happened. The pins that were holding my bones together must have slid out a bit and needed to be put back in. Patience was never my strong suit, so I went over to the nearest pine tree and started banging them back into place – it hurt like hell, but after a few minutes, the pain subsided and the bleeding began to slow.

Mike and I grabbed our bikes and rode back to my house not saying much. We realized that nobody, except for my family, would believe what had happened so we agree to keep it a secret. This is one incident that I never told anyone about until this day.

After that, Mike and I became lifelong friends. We now shared a common bond, having seen with our own eyes, things that were not supposed to happen in the "normal" world.

ENDGAME

Two more years passed uneventfully, almost boring compared to the rest of my life so far. Looking back on it now, I can't say if it was a side effect from the haunting or just plain old teen-age angst, but I soon grew tired of school, almost despising it. I guess with all the family problems and supernatural incidents, school seemed somehow unimportant. I started thinking, what's the point of all this math and science when we don't really know the first thing about the world we live in. A place where things really can go bump in the night – and sometimes during the day too.

Anyway, I ended up getting into a fight with another kid who was making fun of my past experiences. Although I quickly learned to stop talking about such things, there were always some kids who remembered and never lost an opportunity to ridicule.

One day a guy in my class said the wrong thing at the wrong time and I beat him so badly that I was given a choice – expulsion from high school or jail. So, without argument, I left school, much to the dismay of my parents.

Now that I was out of school, my friends would stop by almost daily to hang out, watch TV and drink beer – the typical life of a 17 year old dropout. It was on one of these afternoons that Mike said to me "You know when you asked those questions and the glass answered, well two of the three predictions have come true – you'd better watch out.

I certainly took his advice.

A few months later, my aunt Pat told my mom about a nice piece of land located in upstate New York. The property was just over 20 acres and included a house and a barn. The house was old and rundown, but the barn, big enough for four horses, was in excellent shape. So a few weeks later, my mother and I made a trip to check it out.

It was a beautiful piece of land; the driveway wound its way through a long field which was dotted with old growth pine and oak trees which followed alongside a freshwater stream that was teeming with fish.

When we arrived at the house, we noticed that it wasn't just rundown; it had been partially damaged in a fire. We ventured into town to speak with a local realtor who said that the house had burned down several times over the years. The locals even mentioned that the original house was torched by Indians during a dispute with settlers more than 200 years ago.

I said to my mom, "Seriously, if you buy this place you have to build a new house in a different spot."

Mom nodded in agreement. She told the realtor that we would like to spend some more time there before we made up our mind. We ended up checking into a hotel and spending the next three days examining the property and exploring the surrounding area.

My mother's face would light up each time we visited the farm. As we walked almost every inch of the gorgeous property, she never stopped smiling – it was the first time since the divorce that she seemed truly happy.

That March she signed the papers and the farm was officially hers but she decided to wait until the end of the summer to actually move in, having lots of loose ends to tie up first. She would be starting a new life away from the people she had known and loved for so many years.

And that included Coreen and I. Coreen was now twenty-three and I nineteen. We were doing well in our jobs and had developed ties of our own in the area – Coreen had met a local guy and was engaged to be married.

The summer passed much too quickly as they so often do, and before we knew it, we found ourselves preparing to move our mother and the dogs to the farm. A great friend of mine, Ed Thorn, who was more like family than a friend, agreed to make the five and a half hour journey driving a twenty foot box truck loaded with mom's stuff, while the rest of us, including the two dogs and Jack Daniels, our cat, followed in her car.

Ed, Coreen, and I decided to stay a week and make a family vacation out of it, which turned out to be a great decision. The weather was fantastic – every day was sunny and mild, perfect for things like barbecues and nature walks. Usually in the afternoon, we would drive into Cooperstown, the nearest populated area, to do a little shopping or go to a restaurant.

We helped mom pick out her new modular house and located a nice spot to build it on; down by the stream and next to an ancient stand of oak trees. We all agreed that it would look fantastic and promised to come visit every chance we could.

Finally, after a week of real quality time as a family, everyone except mom piled into the box truck for the trip back home to New Jersey.

A few weeks later, during one of my phone calls with mom, she said that some men were coming out that Saturday to pour the foundation. The house itself should be completed by the end of the week. I told her that Coreen and I would come up as soon as the house was ready to help her unpack. I could hear the happiness in her voice and almost see the smile on her face as I hung up saying, "I love you mom, we all miss you!"

So I was in good spirits later that night as I made my way

to a local party down the road. It was about ten o'clock when I arrived to greet my friends and acquaintances. I drank a couple of beers and had a good time exchanging jokes and stories with some friends, but something was different – I couldn't put my finger on it but I had this anxious feeling like something was going to happen. Then at 11:35pm, without a word to anyone I left the party and walked back home. I couldn't shake the nagging feeling that something wasn't right. I tried to focus on happier thoughts, but there was just an empty feeling of great sadness.

As I arrived home I noticed that the lights were on but the front door was locked. When I opened the door I saw my father's dentures sitting on the coffee table, which was odd since I had no idea that he'd be stopping by. There was no note or message on the answering machine so I assumed that everything must be okay and went off to bed.

However, sleep did not come easy for some reason. Several times during the night I awoke to my own screams, but I couldn't remember the dream that had caused them. I tossed and turned until about seven o'clock the next morning when I got up and went into the kitchen to make some breakfast. As I entered I heard crying coming from the living room. It was Coreen, sobbing uncontrollably. Still groggy, I asked her what had happened. Her fiancé grabbed me by my shoulders and told me to sit down.

"I'm sorry… it's you're mom . . . she died last night… we just got the call."

I ask numbly, "How?"

He replied, "There was a fire… a bad one."

"Where's dad?" I asked.

Coreen answered, "He's in intensive care. I came over last night to check on him but he was just laying on the couch, unresponsive. I found an empty bottle of pain killers and a half empty bottle of scotch."

Her fiancé continued, "We drove him to the hospital as

fast as we could, but he went into a coma almost as soon as we got there."

"What time was that?" I asked.

"According to his medical chart it was 11:38pm."

A cold shiver traveled up my spine, "And mom died around 11:30, didn't she?" I asked.

Coreen answered, "As a matter of fact it was 11:35 pm."

After a few minutes, we managed to get our emotions back under control enough to notify our cousins who in turn spread the news to the rest of the family. We then got in the car and drove to the hospital to see our father. When we arrived, we found him conscious and alert. He showed no surprise when we told him that mom had died.

"I know." he said with tears in his eyes, "She said goodbye to me last night in a dream."

Coreen said, "We have to go now, we're driving to New York to make the funeral arrangements." She kissed him on the forehead and said, "You take care of yourself, okay? We'll see you as soon as we get back."

He replied, "Good luck, I love you." And after a few minutes we were on our way.

For five and a half hours there was no conversation. Occasionally one of us would start crying softly, but mainly we just stared straight ahead, lost in our thoughts.

When we arrived, we could still see the pile of smoldering timbers which was all that remained of the barn. It didn't just burn down, it practically disintegrated. The heat being so intense that the lawn mower inside melted. Everything but the engine block had turned to a puddle of molten metal.

Coreen walked around the site quietly, but I was drawn

inside. As I picked my way through the charred debris, I came upon a gruesome sight – it was the remains of our two dogs. The larger dog had apparently died trying to protect the smaller one by covering it with his body. Now all that remained were the blackened bones and teeth.

Wiping the tears from my eyes, I wandered around aimlessly through the wreckage until something caught my eye – amongst all the blackened debris was a golden necklace surrounding a small object with a reddish sheen to it. Without thinking, I picked it up and wiped off the soot and embers.

Immediately I knew what I had in my hands – it was five vertebrae from my mother's spine. Somehow it was missed and left behind by the coroner. As I held it up, some of the scorched tissue dropped off and a bit of blood oozed from the joints, dripping onto my hands which colored them red.

I don't remember much after that. Coreen said that I just stumbled out of the smoky ruins and fell to my knees, crying and holding the bones up to the heavens, a little trail of blood dripping down my arm.

The next thing I remember, was us traveling to the morgue to identify the body. As soon as we entered we could smell the burnt flesh overpowering the usual chemical odors.

The attendant opened the cooler door and there, on the ice-cold gurney, was what was left of our mother. She was so badly burned that there was almost no muscle or connective tissue left. The coroner had assembled the scorched pieces as best he could – mainly blackened bones and teeth, but it was the skull that would remain in my mind forever.

I gazed at the empty sockets wondering what she saw in those final moments; what her final thoughts might have been. I could only hope that she didn't suffer too much, and was greatly reassured when the coroner, a very kindly fellow, said that she had died of smoke inhalation and likely felt no pain from the fire at all.

However, upon returning to the property, I realized that the coroner had been trying to spare us from any additional grief.

We met the next door neighbor who apologized over and over for not being able to save her.

"I was walking my dog that night around 11:30. I passed by your mother's farm and noticed a light on in the barn and assumed that she was probably out feeding her dogs so I continued on my way. A few minutes later as I was returning, I noticed a bright light in the sky coming from the direction of the farm. As I rounded a corner I could see that the entire barn was engulfed in flames where just a few minutes earlier there was nothing. It was the most intense fire I had ever seen, it must have practically exploded in flames, but I heard nothing – until I got closer, then I heard her screams."

He almost broke down himself while telling us the story, "I'm... I'm so sorry, I couldn't even get near the place – it looked like the inside of a furnace, it... it just wasn't natural!"

I put my hand on his shoulder and nodded, "No, it wasn't natural at all." There was only one thought in my mind now – Enoch, he had done this. I remembered years ago after mom finished the session with the Ouija board. She told us "You won't have to worry about Enoch anymore, he won't be able to hurt you kids." Had this been part of the bargain? Had he followed her hundreds of miles away to collect on this unholy debt? Was this the real reason she had moved so far away in the first place? Was she trying to escape? And what about me? Why was I singled out when he wrote on the walls? Why didn't he threaten to kill me too?

I had no answers; only a million questions that all boiled down to one – Why?

The End

Afterword

Over the years, many families would move into and out of the old house on Hurley Pond Road. Some of them would find that they too, have a story to tell. You have already read about the Richards. They were the first couple to move into the house after my family left, but barely lasted one night before running away in a panic, leaving all of their possessions behind.

Then came the Stefon family; John, his wife Debbie and their five year old son Keith, who was the light of their life. Although they lasted longer than the Richards, their happy family life ended suddenly one hot mid-summer day as the family was lounging around the pool.

Around noon on that sweltering afternoon, Debbie stepped inside for a moment to make sandwiches for lunch, leaving her husband dozing on a lounge chair and Keith playing with his toy cars on the patio nearby. She slapped together three bologna sandwiches in less than two minutes, but by the time she returned to the backyard it was already too late. There, floating face down and motionless in the pool was young Keith. His hysterical parents pulled him from the water and tried desperately to revive him as they waited for the ambulance to arrive, but he never regained consciousness.

John and Debbie were inconsolable. They moved out soon after Keith's funeral, putting the house up for sale once again.

It was eventually purchased by the Daniels, a family of four with some eerie similarities to both my family and some other former tenants – the Baxters.

The father, Warren Daniels, was a tall, six-foot-five engineer. The mother, Donna, who was about my mom's size had two young children, a boy and girl.

They were only in the house for a few weeks when they found a strange message on a wall in the basement. Most of it was unintelligible and only the words "GO AWAY" were legible. At first they thought that it might have been their daughter who had been known to write on everything with her crayons, but these words were done in paint and a seven year old would never be able to get into the locked paint cabinet. Unable to solve the mystery, they quickly cleaned off the graffiti, only to have a similar message appear a few days later.

Shaken by the mysterious incidents, the couple grasped for answers. Confident that no one outside the family had gotten into the house, they carefully searched the wall for some kind of clue, but found nothing unusual. Then, a few days later, the writing was back, this time the words, "YOU KNOW WHAT TO DO" appeared in big black letters. Donna was frightened out of her wits, although Warren seemed unmoved.

"I'll take care of it." he said quietly, and began to walk away.

Donna glared at him. Far from being reassured, her husband's blank stare and unnatural calm made her more afraid than ever.

That night Warren, who rarely even drank beer or wine, began to drink Scotch – straight up. He savored the first small glass and then began to slam back more, one after another.

After about five or six stiff drinks he went back down to the basement, bringing the bottle of Johnny Walker with him. He wandered around unsteadily, gazing bleary-eyed at the walls until he suddenly noticed the words, "DO IT" written on the paneling in front of him. The phrase was repeated over and over in large bold letters, covering the wall from top to bottom. For several seconds he stood motionless, trying to focus his bloodshot eyes. Then, as if in a trance, he reached out to touch the paint – it was still wet. Without a word or change in expression, he returned upstairs to the den where he unlocked the gun cabinet and removed his favorite double-barreled shotgun from the rack before carefully locking the cabinet again.

He stepped outside to the back porch where he sat down on one of the weathered patio chairs and opened the gun for loading. Reaching into his pocket, he removed two 12-gauge shells and carefully fed them into the chambers before snapping the gun shut with a loud click. Holding the weapon in his hands for a moment, he savored the feel of the crisp, cold metal barrels and the smooth wooden stock, worn by generations of use. It had been his father's gun, and his father's father before him – he had always planned to give it to his own son when he was old enough.

He leaned back in his chair and sighed. "Family," he thought – "That's what matters most." He then placed both barrels of the gun in his mouth, reached down and pulled the trigger. Finally, Warren Daniels was at peace as his fears and worries exploded out of the back of his head in a fine red mist.

Two months later, an older couple moved into the House on Hurley Pond Road. Not much is known about them, but after only three weeks, the husband suffered a massive heart attack and died while sitting in the den.

So once again the house went up for sale, and was purchased by a single man by the name of Sam Patterson who stayed in the house for a record eight years. Like many others before him, he also fell in love with the property and had great plans for the house, although none of his ideas were ever realized.

From time to time I would ride by, thinking to myself, how could one man live in that big house all alone. Even after eight years, there was still, barely any furniture, no curtains or lamp shades, just bare light bulbs. Some of the locals would say that when he first moved in he was very polite and thoughtful, just a decent neighbor and all around nice guy. But as time passed he became a recluse who very seldomly stepped outside. In fact when someone would see him and say hello he would just turn, stare at them for several moments, mumble something under his breath and then quickly walk away.

Eventually, Sam disappeared entirely. He had not been seen in several weeks and the mail had begun to pile up to the point where the mailman had to notify the police. Soon two officers arrived and kicked open the back door, only to be greeted by the powerful stench of decay. As they searched the house they eventually came upon Mr. Patterson. He had fastened a rope to the attic rafters, tied the other end around his neck, then stepped through the trapdoor that opened to the second floor hallway. His body had been hanging there for over three weeks and all that was left was a withered, decaying corpse. He left no note.

It was March 18th 1999 and I was preparing to bury my father Barry James Fitzgerald. Although he was still alive, the cancer in his lungs was raging out of control and he was not expected to last the week. I left his side briefly to make the necessary arrangements at Johnson's funeral home – an all too familiar routine. Over the years, sickness, accidents, and family tragedies had made me a steady customer.

So here I was once again, sitting in Mr. Johnson's office, looking over the papers that would ensure my father's smooth transition to the afterlife.

Having signed the last of the documents, I prepared to leave, anxious to get back to my father. But as I began to walk out, Mr. Johnson told me to close the door and sit back down.

As I returned to the chair, Mr. Johnson stood up and leaned forward, his hands on top of his desk. For several seconds, he said nothing and just looked at me over the rim of his wire frame glasses. Then, quite abruptly he asked, "What the hell is going on in that old house of yours Darren? I've been doing this job since I was twenty years old. I am now seventy-six and I have never taken so many corpses out of one place in my entire life."

With a hint of a smile on my face, I replied, "There isn't enough time in the day to even start an explanation, and right now I've got to get back to my father, but one of these days I'll come back, we'll have a drink and I'll tell you the whole crazy story."

I left his office and headed back home, arriving just in time to say goodbye to my father for the last time. He was still conscious when I arrived at his bedside, but I could see in his eyes that he was dying. I sat there quietly, holding his hand, as his breathing slowed, became more shallow, and then stopped completely. I looked over at the clock – it was 11:35pm. Another coincidence I guess.

I sat motionless for several more minutes, lost in my

thoughts. Finally I stood up and said, "Thanks for everything, Dad." and closed his eyes. Fortunately at least one of my parents died peacefully and with their family.

For most of my adult life I made it a point to stay as far away from the old house on Hurley Pond Road as possible. I went on to live a more or less normal life, free from any supernatural incidents, but as this book nears completion, I find that I can no longer work in my study. Whenever I begin to write, I start to hear what sounds like footsteps pacing up and down the hallway or doors opening and closing – a little scary since I know that no one else is in the house at the time.

So here I sit in the cabin of my pickup truck, scratching out the last few pages under the flickering dome light and wondering if telling this story really is such a good idea after all. Years later and miles away, Enoch is still making his presence known. And as the dome light of my car begins to flicker faster, I can't help but wonder . . have I somehow awakened the beast?

ABOUT THE AUTHOR

Darren Fitzgerald was born on the night of January 21st, 1967 in Point Pleasant New Jersey.

His hobbies include swimming, fishing, SCUBA diving and participating in off-road dirt bike racing, despite having broken most of the bones in his arms and/or legs at one time or another.

Having spent the bulk of his childhood living at the house on Hurley Pond Road, Darren went on to develop a lifelong interest of all things supernatural. As a professional artist, his love of the horror genre is reflected in his drawings and sculptures which are mostly dark, but frequently quite humorous.

After high school, Darren continued to hone his skills on projects using a variety of mediums including acrylics, oils, watercolors, pen and ink, clay sculptures, resin molds, signpainting, illustration and custom portraits. Today he works side by side with master artist Jeff Walmsley in the creation of high-end custom artworks etched in sandblasted glass panels.

Darren has taken a year off to document the first portion of his truly extraordinary life. He currently resides in southern New Jersey.

Silver Seas. Com

↳ ~~7/14~~ 7/17

Made in the USA
Charleston, SC
20 January 2010